E. & M.A. RADFORD
DEATH AND THE PROFESSOR

EDWIN ISAAC RADFORD (1891-1973) and MONA AUGUSTA RADFORD (1894-1990) were married in 1939. Edwin worked as a journalist, holding many editorial roles on Fleet Street in London, while Mona was a popular leading lady in musical-comedy and revues until her retirement from the stage.

The couple turned to crime fiction when they were both in their early fifties. Edwin described their collaborative formula as: "She kills them off, and I find out how she done it." Their primary series detective was Harry Manson who they introduced in 1944.

The Radfords spent their final years living in Worthing on the English South Coast. Dean Street Press have republished three of their classic mysteries: *Murder Jigsaw, Murder Isn't Cricket* and *Who Killed Dick Whittington?*

E. & M.A. RADFORD MYSTERIES
Available from Dean Street Press

E. & M.A. RADFORD

DEATH AND THE PROFESSOR

With an introduction by Nigel Moss

DEAN STREET PRESS

Published by Dean Street Press 2020

Copyright © 1961 E. & M.A. Radford

Introduction Copyright © 2020 Nigel Moss

First published in 1961 by Robert Hale

Cover by DSP

ISBN 978 1 913054 95 3

www.deanstreetpress.co.uk

INTRODUCTION

DOCTOR Harry Manson is a neglected figure, unjustly so, amongst Golden Age crime fiction detectives. The creation of husband and wife authors Edwin and Mona Radford, who wrote as E. & M.A. Radford, Manson was their leading series detective featuring in 35 of 38 mystery novels published between 1944 and 1972. He held dual roles as a senior police detective at Scotland Yard and Head of its Crime Forensics Research Laboratory. In 2019 Dean Street Press republished three early novels from the Doctor Manson series—*Murder Jigsaw* (1944), *Murder Isn't Cricket* (1946), and *Who Killed Dick Whittington?* (1947)—titles selected for their strong plots, clever detection and evocative settings. They are examples of Manson at his best, portraying the appealing combination of powerful intellect and reasoning with creative scientific methods of investigation, while never losing awareness and sensitivity concerning the human predicaments encountered.

Having introduced the Radfords to a new readership, Dean Street Press have now released a further three titles, each quite different in approach and style, written during the authors' middle period but retaining the traditions of the Golden Age of Detective Fiction. They include two Manson novels: *The Heel of Achilles* (1950), an inverted murder mystery; and *Death of a Frightened Editor* (1959), a baffling murder by poisoning on a London-to-Brighton train. The third, *Death and the Professor* (1961), is a non-series title featuring an array of impossible crime puzzles and locked room murders solved by the formidable mind of logician Professor Marcus Stubbs.

The Radfords sought to combine in Doctor Manson a leading police detective and scientific investigator in the same mould as R. Austin Freeman's Dr John Thorndyke, whom Edwin Radford keenly admired. T.J. Binyon, in his study of fictional detectives *Murder Will Out* (1989), maintains that the Radfords were protesting against the idea that in Golden Age crime fiction science is always the preserve of the amateur detective, and were seeking to be different. In the preface to the first Manson novel *Inspector Manson's Success* (1944), they announced: "We have had the audacity to present here the Almost Incredible: a detective story in which the scientific deduction by a police officer uncovers the crime and the criminal entirely without the aid of any outside assistance!"

The first two Manson novels, *Inspector Manson's Success* and *Murder Jigsaw* (both 1944), contain introductory prefaces which acquaint the reader with Doctor Manson in some detail. He is a man of many talents and qualifications: aged in his early 50s and a Cambridge MA (both attributes shared by Edwin Radford at the time), Manson is a Doctor of Science, Doctor of Laws, non-practising barrister and author of several standard works on medical jurisprudence (of which he is a Professor) and criminal pathology. Slightly over 6 feet in height, although he does not look it owing to the stoop of his shoulders, habitual in a scholar and scientist. He has interesting features and characteristics: a long face, with a broad and abnormally high forehead; grey eyes wide set, though lying deep in their sockets, which "have a habit of just passing over a person on introduction; but when that person chances to turn in the direction of the Inspector, he is disconcerted to find that the eyes have returned to his face and are seemingly engaged on long and careful scrutiny. There is left the impression that one's face is being photographed on the Inspector's mind." Manson's hands are often the first thing a stranger will notice. "The long delicate fingers are exceedingly restless—twisting and turning on anything which lies handy to them. While he stands, chatting, they are liable to stray to a waistcoat pocket and emerge with a tiny magnifying glass or a micrometer to occupy their energy."

During his long career at Scotland Yard, Manson rises from Chief Detective-Inspector to the rank of Commander. Reporting directly to Sir Edward Allen, the Assistant Commissioner, Manson is ably assisted by his Yard colleagues—Sergeant Merry, a science graduate and Deputy Lab Head, and Superintendent Jones and Detective-Inspector Kenway of the CID. Jones is weighty and ponderous, given to grunts and short staccato sentences, and with a habit of lapsing into American 'tec slang in moments of stress; but a stolid, determined detective and reliable fact searcher with an impressive memory. He often serves as a humorous foil to Manson and the Assistant Commissioner. By contrast, Kenway is volatile and imaginative. Together, Jones and Kenway make a powerful combination and an effective resource for the Doctor. In later books, Inspector Holroyd features as Manson's regular assistant. Holroyd is the lead detective in the non-series title *The Six Men* (1958), a novelisation of the earlier British detective film of the same name released in 1951 and based on an original story idea and scenario developed by the Radfords. Their only other non-series police detective, Superintendent Carmichael, appeared in just two novels: *Look in at Murder* (1956, with Manson) and *Married to Murder* (1959).

The first eight novels, all Manson series, were published by Andrew Melrose between 1944 to 1950. The early titles were slim volumes produced in accordance with authorised War Economy Standards. Many featured a distinctive motif on the front cover of the dust wrapper—a small white circle showing Manson's head superimposed against that of Sherlock Holmes (in black silhouette), with the title 'a Manson Mystery'. In these early novels, the Radfords made much of their practice of providing readers with all the facts and clues necessary to give them a fair opportunity of solving the mystery puzzles by deduction. They interspersed the investigations with 'Challenges to the Reader', a trope closely associated with leading Golden Age crime authors John Dickson Carr and Ellery Queen. In *Murder Isn't Cricket* they claimed: "We have never 'pulled anything out of the bag' at the last minute—a fact upon which three distinguished reviewers of books have commented and have commended." Favourable critical reviews of their early titles were received from Ralph Straus (*Sunday Times*) and George W. Bishop (*Daily Telegraph*), as well as novelist Elizabeth Bowen. The Radfords were held in sufficiently high regard by Sutherland Scott, in his study of the mystery novel *Blood in their Ink* (1953), to be highlighted alongside such distinguished Golden Age authors as Miles Burton, Richard Hull, Milward Kennedy and Vernon Loder.

After 1950 there was a gap of six years before the Radfords' next book. Mona's mother died in 1953; she had been living with them at the time. Starting in 1956, with a new publisher John Long (like Melrose, another Hutchinson company), the Radfords released two Manson titles in successive years: *Look in at Murder* (1956) and *Death on the Broads* (1957). In 1958 they moved to the publisher Robert Hale, a prominent supplier to the public libraries. They began with *The Six Men* (1958), before returning to Manson with *Death of a Frightened Editor* (1959). Thereafter, Manson was to feature in all but two of their remaining 25 crime novels, all published by Hale; the exceptions being *Married to Murder* (1959) and *Death of a Professor* (1961). Curiously, a revised and abridged version of the third Manson series novel *Crime Pays No Dividends* (1945) was later released under the new title *Death of a Peculiar Rabbit* (1969).

Edwin Isaac Radford (1891-1973) and Mona Augusta Radford (1894-1990) were married in Aldershot in 1939. Born in West Bromwich, Edwin had spent his working life entirely in journalism, latterly in London's Fleet Street where he held various editorial roles, culminating as Arts Editor-in-Chief and Columnist for the *Daily Mirror* in 1937. Mona was the daughter of Irish poet and actor James Clarence Mangan and his actress wife Lily Johnson. Since childhood she had toured with her mother and performed on stage under the name 'Mona Magnet', and later was for many years a popular leading lady appearing in musical-comedies, revues and pantomime (including 'Dick Whittington') until her retirement from the stage. She first met Edwin while performing in Nottingham, where he was working as a local newspaper journalist. Mona also authored numerous short plays and sketches for the stage, in addition to writing verse, particularly for children.

An article in *Books & Bookmen* magazine (1959) recounts how Edwin and Mona, already in their early 50s, became detective fiction writers by accident. During one of Edwin's periodic attacks of lumbago, Mona trudged through snow and slush from their village home to a library for Dr Thorndyke detective stories by R. Austin Freeman, of which he was an avid reader. Unfortunately, Edwin had already read the three books with which she returned! Incensed at his grumbles, Mona retaliated with "Well for heaven's sake, why don't you write one instead of always reading them?"—and placed a writing pad and pencil on his bed. Within a month, Edwin had written six lengthy short stories, and with Mona's help in revising the MS, submitted them to a leading publisher. The recommendation came back that each of the stories had the potential to make an excellent full-length novel. The first short story was duly turned into a novel, which was promptly accepted for publication. Thereafter, their practice was to work together on writing novels—first in longhand, then typed and read through by each of them, and revised as necessary. The plot was usually developed by Mona and added to by Edwin during the writing. According to Edwin, the formula was: "She kills them off, and I find out how she done it." Mona would also act the characters and dialogue as outlined by Edwin for him to observe first-hand and then capture in the text.

As husband-and-wife novelists, the Radfords were in the company of other Golden Age crime writing couples—G.D.H. (Douglas) and Margaret Cole in the UK, and Gwen Bristow and Bruce Manning, John and Emery Bonett, Audrey and Wiliam Roos (Kelley Roos), and Frances and Richard Lockridge in the USA. Their crime novels proved popular on the Continent and were published in translation in the major European languages. However, the US market eluded them and none of the Radford books was ever published in the USA. Aside from crime fiction, the Radfords collaborated on authoring a wide range of other works, most notably *Crowther's Encyclopaedia of Phrases and Origins*, *Encyclopaedia of Superstitions* (a standard work on folklore), and a *Dictionary of Allusions*. Edwin was a Fellow of the Royal Society of Arts, and a member of both the Authors' Club and the Savage Club.

The Radfords proved to be an enduring writing team, working into their 80s. Both were also enthusiastic amateur artists in oils and water colours. They travelled extensively, and invariably spent the winter months writing in the warmer climes of Southern Europe. An article by Edwin in *John Creasey's Mystery Bedside Book* (1960) recounts his involvement in the late 1920s with an English society periodical for the winter set on the French Riviera, where he had socialised with such famous writers as Baroness Orczy, William Le Queux and E. Phillips Oppenheim. He recollects Oppenheim dictating up to three novels at once! The Radfords spent their final years living in Worthing.

Death and the Professor

The Radfords were innovators. They frequently devised original methods of committing murder, for example in *It's Murder to Live* (1947) and *John Kyeling Died* (1949). In their unusual, one-off work *Death and the Professor*, the entire book is based around the Dilettantes Club, an exclusive London dining club, and the varied crime cases which are solved during discussions among its members, thanks to the insights of the eponymous Professor, Marcus Stubbs. For this mid-period title, published in 1961 by Robert Hale, the authors rest their principal series detective Doctor Manson, and introduce Professor Stubbs who makes his sole appearance as the protagonist. But Manson's CID colleagues Detective-Inspector Kenway and Superintendent Jones feature in reports on police investigations. Moreover, Sir Edward Allen, Assistant Commissioner at Scotland Yard (to whom Manson reports), plays a key role in the book as one of the Club members, and his professional abilities and prowess shine through in the finale.

The Dilettantes Club is made up of a handful of leading savants, including Sir Edward, drawn from medicine, science and academia. Initially five members, they are joined at the outset of the book by Professor Stubbs, a former Professor of Logic at Bonn University, and the holder of a doctorate in philosophy from the Sorbonne. Stubbs has memorable characteristics: he is an elderly, thin man with a goblin-like head, shock of grey hair, thick lensed heavy spectacles, aged dress suit, a snuff taker, pedantic in his manner of speech with a frequent stammer, and generally possessing a hesitant, mild-mannered persona. Aspects of his appearance and demeanour are similar to those of Jacques Futrelle's earlier fictional creation Professor Augustus S.F.X. Van Dusen (also a logician), better known to mystery readers as "The Thinking Machine". The Club meets fortnightly in a private dining room of Moroni's restaurant in Soho. The authors lovingly detail the lavish gourmet dinners and fine wines consumed before the members get down to the more serious business of the evening, discussing crime problems around the dining table over coffee, liqueurs and cigars.

The book comprises eight stand-alone short stories. The writing style suggests they may originally have been conceived for serialisation. Seven of the eight stories are a mix of impossible crimes and locked room mystery stories; the remaining story is a cleverly plotted 'eternal triangle' murder. The authors' enjoyment of the popular locked room mystery sub-genre is evident, with a variety of baffling cases including death by shooting in a locked guest house room; an induced heart attack in a locked railway carriage; and strangulation in a guarded flat. The Radfords wrote two other impossible crime novels: *Who Killed Dick Whittington?* (1947) and *Death of a Frightened Editor* (1959), both reissued by Dean Street Press. Doctor Manson also discusses a theoretical locked room murder scenario in *The Heel of Achilles* (1950).

The eight stories are presented individually to the Club members for debate by the Assistant Commissioner, Sir Edward Allen; they feature brain-teasing problems of criminal investigations that have baffled the police. In one instance it is the Professor who raises the case to prevent what he suspects to be a grave miscarriage of justice. But the Professor does not normally initiate discussion; his habit is to be the last member to offer any contribution, after first analysing all the facts and discussions. With his eyes closed and head shrunk between the shoulders, the members are never sure whether the Professor is awake or asleep. But on finally entering the fray, he follows an apparent process of reasoning based on strict logic, often quite elaborate and demonstrating an impressive attention to detail. The Professor evaluates and sifts the evidence, plugging gaps in the existing police investigation findings, and concludes by successfully pointing the finger at those who are evading justice. His summations often prove embarrassing for the police. But in a surprising denouement the authors introduce a masterful final twist, and Sir Edward has the last laugh.

Upon publication of *Death and the Professor*, the *Manchester Evening Chronicle* wrote: "Another treat for addicts. Once again they (the authors) succeed in holding the reader's interest by combining an ingenious plot with a collection of really convincing characters". The eye-catching dust wrapper of the Robert Hale first edition features a street scene (probably London) with a life-like picture of the Professor wearing black formal attire and the dark figure of an over-sized skeleton, similarly dressed, looming behind him. This new edition by Dean Street Press, almost sixty years later, will be particularly welcomed by the many collectors and fans of impossible crimes and locked room mysteries for whom the book has been difficult to locate. The varied problems in the book's stories occupy a full page of Robert Adey's leading reference work *Locked Room Murders* (1991).

The Dilettantes Club and the private dinner meetings of its members form the backdrop of the whole book. Anthony Lejeune wrote that the Club milieu provides a setting "useful to the mystery writer in constituting an accidental meeting place and a jumping-off point for adventures, serving as an indicator of social status, and providing a nostalgic quality beloved of many readers of mysteries." Edwin Radford was a member of the Savage Club, a leading Bohemian Gentleman's Club in London. Other classic Golden Age mysteries in which clubs feature prominently include Dorothy L. Sayers's *The Unpleasantness at the Belladonna Club* (1927); John Dickson Carr's *The Lost Gallows* (1931)—the Brimstone Club; Richard Hull's *Keep it Quiet* (1935)—the Whitehall Club, and *The Murderers of Monty* (1937)—the Pall Mall Club; and Miles Burton's *Death at the Club* (1937)—the Witchcraft Club. Earlier, the Diogenes Club had served as the setting in which Arthur Conan Doyle first introduced Mycroft Holmes, brother of Sherlock. But there are two further Club milieu titles which have closer parallels with *Death and the Professor*, namely Anthony Berkeley's *The Poisoned Chocolates Case* (1929) and later Isaac Asimov's *Tales of the Black Widowers* (1974).

Julian Symons called *The Poisoned Chocolate Case* "one of the most cunning trick shows in the history of detective fiction". The novel was expanded from Berkeley's excellent short story 'The Avenging Chance'. It features the Crimes Circle, an exclusive London club formed of six amateur criminologists who meet over dinners to discuss criminous matters. The Crimes Circle has similarities with the real-life Detection Club which

Berkeley helped to form in 1930. The members of the Circle are invited by a Scotland Yard Chief-Inspector to deliberate informally on a murder-by-poisoning case which the police have been unable to solve. Each member individually propounds a different solution. But it is the last member to speak, Mr Ambrose Chitterwick, who provides the correct explanation, using the clues that the five other members had misinterpreted to expose the real poisoner. In appearance and demeanour, Mr Chitterwick is a little, mild-mannered and seemingly ineffectual man; in fact he is highly astute and possesses a keen eye for detail. There are certain similarities between the Crimes Circle and the Dilettantes Club as well as Mr Chitterwick and Professor Stubbs. Berkeley also featured Mr Chitterwick in two subsequent detective novels, *The Piccadilly Murder* (1929) and *Trial and Error* (1937).

Isaac Asimov created The Black Widowers, a fictional dining club set in New York, which appears in a series of sixty-six mystery stories that he started writing at the beginning of the 1970s, mostly for *Ellery Queen's Mystery Magazine*. The Black Widowers is based on a literary dining club, The Trap Door Spiders, to which Asimov belonged. The first and best-known of six short story collections is *Tales of the Black Widowers* (1974). The six members of the Black Widowers club meet once a month in a private room of Milano's restaurant in Manhattan. The stories adopt the same pattern and structure, with the members taking it in turn to act as host and invite a guest to a club dinner. They are served by Milano's revered head steward Henry, who is treated as a de facto member. The guests raise various problems, mostly criminous, which the members then discuss and try to solve. Invariably they fail to reach a conclusion, and it is Henry who provides the correct answer, deduced from the details which had emerged during the preceding conversations. Asimov also wrote the Union Club mysteries; short stories which are similar to the Black Widowers but shorter. While better known for his Science Fiction, Asimov was fond of impossible crime detection puzzles and wrote several novels and short stories which successfully combine both genres, most notably *The Caves of Steel* (1954) and *The Naked Sun* (1957).

Nigel Moss

THE Dilettantes' Club meets on the first and last Thursday of each month (except in August, when the members are scattered for their holidays). At 7 p.m. the chairman, Sir Noël Maurice, rises from his chair at the head of the table, and proposes 'The Queen,' for the members are all elderly, and maintain still that graciousness of life which mostly passed after the First World War, and one unwritten law of which requires that a company of gentlemen dining together shall wear dinner jackets and black bows; at 10.30 p.m. he rises again with a bow and a 'good night' to each member; after which the company disperses until the calendar has revolved another fortnight.

The Dilettantes are exactly what the name implies: wanderers among the Arts and Sciences. Each is a doyen of his own particular profession. There is Sir Noël himself, Knight of the most Excellent Order of the British Empire, in his middle sixties, a surgeon of international stature, and one of the world's greatest authorities on the heart. There is Sir Edward Allen, Assistant Commissioner of Scotland Yard, whose fervent belief in Science as a weapon against crime led to his founding a Crime Laboratory in Scotland Yard itself. Norman Charles, another member, is an authority on the human mind — a psychiatrist, also of international repute — a tubby man with eyes which seem always to be calculating his *vis-à-vis* in conversation — and probably are. And there is Alexander Purcell, whose figurings and jugglings weigh up the welfare of industry and of nations: he is a mathematician, a Senior Wrangler of Cambridge, holder of Mathematical Tripos, and a Chair in Mathematics.

Fifth of the Dilettantes in order of joining, is William James. Where Sir Noël works for life, Mr. James deals in death: he is a pathologist, delving into the passage to Eternity of those who did not expect, or were not expected, to make the journey so soon.

These, then, are the original Dilettantes — a surgeon, a policeman, a psychiatrist, a mathematician and a pathologist: as varied a selection of brains as one could expect to find gathered round a table for the purpose of browsing among the bric-à-brac of events and happenings in the world around them, the bizarre and the mysterious, the riddles of living and dying. Since one and all valued gastronomy as one of the major Arts of mankind, it was inevitable that their meeting place should be Moroni's: for Moroni's, as everybody who is anybody knows, is the dining Mecca of all who aspire to the reputation of gourmets.

There is a sixth Dilettante, who joined the company a considerable time after its formation. The manner of his coming was curious. There is no reference to the club in the list of London clubs, nor has it a number in the London telephone directory. The only outward and visible sign of its existence is a small brass plate, three inches by one inch affixed to the inside of a lintel of the entrance to Moroni's, which is in Soho. The club dines and debates in the Lucullus Room, on the first floor of the restaurant.

It is the rule that when the dinner is ended, the table cleared and the port and cigars laid out, there shall not on any pretext be any outside interruptions to the debating. It was, therefore, remarkable that on a warm evening in July, a discussion on the Infinitesimal Calculus should have been halted at its most intriguing point — which of the labours of Descartes, Newton or Leibniz had added greatest to the mathematical formulae of Archimedes: Newton through systematic foundation or Calculus, or Descartes's 'Geometrie' and his 'Method' and Ontological argument — by a sudden appearance in the open doorway of a stranger.

Their conversation cut off, the five stared at him. Purcell, caught with his right index finger in mid-air pointing a submission, let it drop slowly to the table. They saw a little man some 5 feet 7 inches in height, who was gesturing uncertainties. He had a goblin-like shock of hair on his big head, and peered behind gig-like spectacles.

'I . . . I . . . am s-sorry to disturb you gentlemen,' he announced. 'I d . . . did knock, but you perhaps did not hear me.' He paused to gain breath lost in the climb up the stairs. 'Could . . . I . . . see the secretary, please?'

The five rose in courtesy. 'Come inside, sir, and close the door,' Sir Noël invited. 'Give our visitor a chair, James.' He waited until the little man was settled. Then: 'Mr. Purcell is the keeper of our archives, sir. We have no secretary. What can we do for you?'

'Ah!' The visitor peered through his thick glasses. 'I thought I recognized you, Mr. Purcell. We are already slightly acquainted.'

The mathematician looked closely. The visitor wore a dinner jacket of considerable vintage, cut very square and turning a rusty brown in places, and with a waistcoat reaching almost up to the breast. He had an obvious 'dicky' in place of a boiled shirt. 'Are we, sir?' he queried.

'Yes. We met at Oxford some years ago — at the University: in the house of the Master of Oriel.'

The chairman broke into the reminiscence. 'But that would not explain your visit to us, Mr —?'

'Stubbs — Marcus Stubbs.'

'— Mr. Stubbs. What can we do for you?'

'I had the intention, and the hope, of joining the club.'

Eight startled eyes turned to the chairman. Sir Noël fingered his moustache, and hemmed a little. 'I am afraid we are not admitting new members, Mr. Stubbs,' he said. 'There are, in any case, certain requirements. What, for instance, are you in, shall I say scholarship?'

'I am a logician.'

'Ah,' Mr. Purcell broke in. 'I remember now. Bonn.'

The visitor nodded.

'I was Professor of Logic at Bonn, at the time — yes. I resigned my chair to write a treatise. *Ein esel ein Eisel!* I still am writing.' He saw the doubts in the faces of his hosts. 'I, too, am a dilettante,' he said. 'I wander amidst the labyrinth of thought, its processes and arguments. I take apart the fallacies of society. In the realm of philosophy I have a Doctorate of the Sorbonne.'

The chairman fingered his moustache and looked round the Dilettantes. They whispered together. Then: 'Would you mind retiring to the service room' — he indicated the door — 'while we discuss this unusual situation?' Mr. Stubbs went.

Inside the Dilettantes looked at each other, and at the Chairman Sir Noël hemmed. 'This is an embarrassing situation,' he said. 'How on earth did the man hear of the club?'

James wrinkled his brows. 'He looks a little scruffy to me. Not that —'

'No, that does not matter.' The chairman completed the sentence. 'We are concerned only with intellect.' He turned to Purcell: 'Have you any knowledge of him?' he asked.

'Yes. I know — or rather knew — of him by repute. The Master of Balliol invited him to pay a visit to the University. The Master himself had been immensely impressed by a paper he had written on philosophy with applied logical reasoning, hence the invitation. I remember he had dinner with the Master and several Dons. I was not present, having a previous engagement, but I joined the company afterwards. He stayed only that one night and then returned to Bonn. There was no doubt about his scholarship and his reputation. I saw him only for an hour or so, in the soft lights of the Master's room, and certainly would not have recognized him now, had he not reminded me of the occasion. It was, you understand, quite a few years ago.'

There was a pause. The chairman considered the situation with furrowed brows. Purcell interposed on his thoughts. 'If you like, Noël, I will have a word over the telephone with Sir John. He is not, of course, Master now, but he lives in Kensington.' The chairman nodded, and Purcell crossed to the telephone.

The conversation lasted some three or four minutes. Purcell replaced the receiver, and nodded. 'Sir John agrees with me as to his visit,' he announced. 'A little man with a pedantic manner of speech, he described him, but with a brilliant brain. That seems to fit our visitor. He has not heard of him for some years, except casually. But he recalled that he gave up his Chair for personal reasons. The Chancellor of Bonn, who had tried to dissuade him, said the reason he gave was something about research along a new line of thought in philosophy. It led, by the way, to the Doctorate at the Sorbonne. His own view is that Stubbs would be an ornament to any gathering of savants — in an intellectual sense.'

'Well, that seems satisfactory from that point of view,' the chairman said. 'The point is do we want to increase our membership? Are there any objections to another member — of erudition?'

There was a general shaking of heads. Mr. James broke in: 'It might be advantageous to our company to possess the mechanics of a logical process of thinking, and a decree of pure philosophy.'

The chairman nodded. 'Shall we take a vote on it?' Four hands were raised and the chairman joined them. The visitor was recalled.

'Mr. Stubbs,' the chairman said, 'we have decided to welcome you amongst us.' He shook hands. 'We look forward to benefiting our discussions from your attainments and knowledge.' He looked at his watch. 'It is now 10.30 and our time for breaking up. We hope — and indeed look forward with pleasure — to seeing you at our next meeting.'

2

WITH the table cleared of its burden of Georgian silver — the gift to each other of the Dilettantes — the port and cigars laid out, and the waiter out of the room, Sir Noël Maurice cleared his throat, and addressed the company. That was the unchanging formula: until the meal was ended and the members could relax, talk was confined to a minimum; it was a *sine qua non* that the mental activity of sustained conversation robbed the connoisseur of the ability fully to enjoy the culinary achievement placed in front of him. But that over, there began the real business of the club — the battle of wits and learning which was the *raison d'être* for the Dilettantes.

'To-night's problem for discussion comes from Sir Edward,' the chairman announced. 'As you will expect, it concerns crime; and it is a very intriguing problem, indeed.' He turned to the newest Dilettante. 'I should explain, Professor, that the rule is to allow the speaker to state his case without interruption, except for such interjections as are necessary to elucidate any particular point, and then general examination of the facts, and a discussion.' The professor nodded. 'Very well, Sir Edward, the table is yours.'

The Assistant Commissioner of Scotland Yard took a sip from his port and lighted a cigar. He fingered his monocle on its black silk ribbon, and began: 'It is, as Sir Noël has indicated, an intriguing case, and one which for the moment has my men completely fogged.' He paused and turned his cigar between his fingers, eyeing, appreciatively, the levelness of the burning. 'For the beginning I must take you to a boarding house — The Lodge Guest House, in Coronation Road, South Kensington: a Victorian-style house with stone steps up to the front door, railings in front, and stone steps going down to a basement. You all know the kind of house and street; they are common enough in South Ken, which has fallen from the high estate it once boasted.

'The landlady is a Mrs. Sophie Leeming, but she plays no part in the affair, and can be forgotten. At the time of the occurrence the house had nine residents. They were Mrs. Amelia Anstruther, elderly, and the widow of a doctor who left her comfortably off; Colonel Harry Parmenter, aged 68, retired infantry commander; Mr. Francis Bristow, with no occupation; Major Will Piedmont, also retired from the army; Miss Maudie Mackinder, a rather flighty young woman of 26; Miss Lorna Mentrose, elderly and independent; Miss Alicia Rose, the same; Mr. Alan Norris, a newcomer — he had lived there just a week — of no occupation; and Mr. Frederick Banting, aged about 50, a business man who had a single room in a block of offices in Crown Court, off Fleet Street. And there was Mary, the maid servant.

'It is with Banting that we are chiefly concerned. He was the misfit in the hackneyed phrase, genteel, but in reduced circumstances, with the exception of Mr. Norris, who was younger. Banting was loud voiced and coarse, rude to everybody, and with a complete disregard for the pleasantries and courtesies of life in company. He was cordially disliked by one and all. If he is to be believed he was a man for the ladies.'

The A.C. took another sip of port and smelled appreciatively the aroma of his cigar. He settled more comfortably in his chair, and then continued: 'At 7 o'clock on Monday evening — that is four days ago — all nine residents were sitting at tables in the hall-lounge. Dinner had been at 6.15 and coffee was now being served. At ten minutes past seven Mr. Banting noisily replaced his cup in its saucer, rose, and shuffled a rude and pushing way between the chairs and tables of the other guests, to the foot of the staircase. The company followed his progress with resentful glances, and watched him disappear by degrees — from his head downwards to the boot of his right foot — which was the last piece of the live Banting they were ever to see.

'With his passing out of sight tension fell upon the company. Talk ceased and all ears were attuned as though expecting something to happen, explosively. I am, I should tell you, describing the atmosphere gathered by my investigating officers later. The expected happened! A loud bang reverberated through the house shaking the windows and rattling ornaments on the piano (which, by the way, had never been played or even opened within the memory of any of the residents). Mr. Banting had entered his room. It seems he always banged the door that way — morning, noon and midnight. The general opinion was that he did so deliberately, to annoy his fellow guests or, as he called them, according the flighty Miss Mackinder, 'the 'igh and mighty 'as-beens and their mutton dressed up as lamb'.

'The expected having duly happened the lounge once more rippled into small talk, rising and falling like the ebb and flow of waves on a shingle shore. The waiter, a decrepit figure in a grease-motleyed tails suit was collecting the coffee cups.'

Sir Edward paused and leaned forward to refill his glass. The Dilettantes were listening to his précis with attention so studied that the cigars of two of them had gone out; they seized the opportunity to relight them. The A.C. waited for them to puff up, and then continued.

'I must now digress for a moment to present to you the position and situation inside and outside the house. The reason will be apparent later. Well, then, it was a beautiful July evening at 7.15 with the sun still shining warmly. In the street, directly outside the house one of London's three remaining barrel-organs was grinding out 'Sweet Rosie O'Grady'; we know that because Mrs. Anstruther says she was listening to it nostalgically. One of the organ's crew was turning the handle; the other was watching doors and windows for any 'appreciation'. He was actually watching the front window over the door, because he had seen a man standing at it a moment before. This, by the way, was Banting's window. There is no back to the house, other than a small square yard which backs on to a similar yard of the opposite house in a parallel street. A high wall divides them.

'Inside, in the lounge were the eight guests, and the waiter; upstairs, Mary, the maid, was turning down the beds. In the basement kitchen, Mrs. Leeming, the land-lady, was washing-up the dinner things, helped by an evening woman. That was the set-up at 7.20 o'clock, five minutes after Banting had gone to his room and banged the door.

'Then it happened! From upstairs there came, start-lingly, a second bang. The unexpectedness of it chopped off the gossip literally in the middle of words, and (so Mrs.

Anstruther says) jumped twelve stitches off the needles on which she was knitting a modestly grey jumper. It also betrayed her, Miss Mackinder asserts into a loud 'damn'; and this will probably be held against her for the remainder of her stay in Coronation Road, she being a consistent church-goer. However, she stormed up in her annoyance with, '*Now* what's the man banging?'

Colonel Parmenter had shot out of his chair at the explosion. 'That wasn't a bang,' he said. 'That was a shot.' He should know, being an old infantry officer. He moved towards the stairs. 'A revolver shot,' he augmented. 'Come along, you men!'

Sir Edward felt in an inside pocket and brought out a slim writing pad. He adjusted his monocle in his left eye and read over his notes. 'I want to get this quite accurate,' he apologized. 'The colonel led the men to the first floor corridor from which four bedrooms opened. The maid, scared half out of her wits, peeped white-faced, round the turning at the farther end. 'It came from Mr. Banting's room, Colonel,' she called out. 'Whatever was it?' The colonel rapped on a panel of the door. 'Are you all right, Banting?' he called. There was no reply. He knocked again, heavily. No sound came from within. The door-handle turned in his grasp, but the door remained closed. The colonel knelt down and peered at the keyhole.

'No key in it,' he said. 'Give me your master key, Mary.' The girl brought it, and scuttled back to the corner. The colonel inserted the key in the lock and turned it. He threw open the door, and the group rushed into the room after joggling each other in the doorway. There they stopped.

'*Banting lay on the floor. Blood was spreading slowly over the carpet. A revolver lay beside him.*

'The colonel bent down and lifted his head. He let it drop again, and stood up. 'Better get out, men,' he said.

'He's shot through the head. Quite dead. I'll telephone the police! He locked the door, and put the key in a pocket. The last thing he noticed was the barrel organ; it was playing, rather inappropriately 'Let me like a soldier fall'.'

3

THE company were following the narrative with an interest that was eloquently illustrated in their attitudes. Sir Noël Maurice was bending forward in his chair, elbows on the table. Both Charles and James had concentrated so intently that they had committed the unpardonable sin of allowing a good cigar again to become dead. The Dilettantes were accustomed to absorbing problems from Sir Edward but this one, was by general consent better than most. Purcell, the mathematician, was slouched back in his seat with eyes closed. He opened them as the A.C. finished speaking.

'But that isn't all?' he suggested.

'Not by any means,' Sir Edward agreed. 'I want refreshment.' He smiled and swallowed some port. 'Well, then, Detective-Inspector Kenway and a sergeant were at Coronation Road within ten minutes after the 999 call. The eight residents were in the lounge, bringing the landlady out of hysterics. The inspector, after viewing the body took their statements; it is from those that I have compiled this precis. Then he went back to the bedroom, with his sergeant.

'Banting's body was lying between the door and the bed, and facing the window. There was a bullet wound in his right temple, and an exit wound at the back of the head. He had obviously died instantly. The weapon was on the floor, on his right side, about two feet from the body — an automatic of French make, 7.63 —'

'His own?' the Pathologist asked. The A.C. nodded. 'He kept it in a drawer of his desk. Mary, the maid, who seems a bit of a snooper, announced that she had seen it there on several occasions.' The A.C. smiled slightly. 'The statement brought indignant stares from the woman guests and a strangled word from the landlady. The snooper seemed in for trouble. Incidentally, Banting had no licence for the automatic.

'The inspector spent twenty minutes in the room. He called up Mary and the decrepit waiter to whom he put a request which was complied with. Then he telephoned me from the squad car, and asked for the help of the Murder Squad.

Five pairs of eyes turned, startled, on the A.C. Only the voice of two of them spoke — the professor:

'W . . . why m . . . murder?' he asked.

'The appearance of the room.' The A.C. felt in his inside pocket. 'I have copies of sketches which Inspector Kenway made of the room and its contents. You may like to examine them.' He passed them round.

The club members studied the sketches. Sir Edward lighted another cigar — and waited.

'Nothing?' he queried when they looked up again. 'Ah, well it is of no consequence.'

'And the Murder Squad?' asked James, who was the pathologist. 'I am impatient.'

'The room was combed all through. It and everything it contained were finger-printed. There were prints only of Banting and the maid — on the bed framework, the desk, the bedside table, on the chairs, wardrobe and chest of drawers — and no other prints. On the automatic there were only Banting's fingers. Banting's key to his room was on the writing desk where, presumably, he had put it when he had locked his bedroom door on entering. I should add that he had a phobia about locking his room. The Squad found no sign of struggle, or even disturbance. The only thing out of order was the left-hand drawer in the desk; it had been forced — judging by the marks — with a steel paper-knife lying on the desk. The blade bore Banting's prints. Inside it was a brief-size leather carrying wallet. It was empty. Mary, who snooped, said that whenever she was in the room when Banting was writing, the wallet was always on top of the desk, and was always full of papers.'

'So Banting was murdered?' The query came from the chairman. The A.C. smiled, gently.

'Ah! I did not say so. There's the rub. We don't know whether he was, or not. I will pick the wealth of brains and reasoning round this table. Tell me, did he commit suicide, or was he killed in his room; and if so how a murderer killed and vanished leaving no trace within a minute?'

4

SIR Noël Maurice, from the chair gazed benignly round the company and chuckled. 'Admirable,' he said and his voice had the timbre of delight. 'Quite the best problem to come before the Dilettantes.' He nodded to the A.C. 'Our thanks to you, Edward . . . Well, who starts the ball rolling?' His eyes wandered over their faces . . . 'Purcell!'

The mathematician smiled. 'X is the unknown quantity,' he said. 'Let us equate. We have a total of nine people. Can we reduce? . . . Say, on alibis?'

'The eight guests alibi each other,' the A.C. said. 'They agree they were together in the lounge when the shot was fired. They were together when Banting was found, the men upstairs, the women on the stairs looking up. The landlady has the evening help as her alibi.'

'Between the sound of the shot and the arrival of the men at the door of the room, how long?'

'We tested it by a repeat performance — two minutes.'

The psychiatrist interposed. 'The human mind and its sudden reflexes are unaccountable. There is here the too obvious, which, however, is sometimes the unexpected truth. There is one person upstairs, a maid. There is Banting, said to be a man for the ladies. Postulate the maid turning down the bed . . . an overture . . . a repulse. Then persistence, and the mind panics. She backs away — to the desk. She knows there is a revolver there. She takes it and points it. Her finger tenses, and it explodes. She darts to the door, locks it from the outside with her master-key and peers at the running men from the corner of the corridor. It could be done in two minutes but that is not murder.'

The A.C. nodded. Then he smiled. 'Banting stood 6 ft. 1 in.: Mary 5ft. 5 ins.,' he responded. 'The bullet entered the head horizontally. Unless she was standing on a chair she could not have fired that shot.'

Sir Noël said: 'It was a very warm evening. The window, perhaps, was open. A watcher across the street —'

'The window was closed and, in fact, locked with a thumb-screw. Banting had a fear of burglary,' the A.C. said.

The professor had been peering over the sketches for three or four minutes. There was an air of absorption about him, and he had taken no part in the discussion. The chairman called his name twice before he looked up and became aware of the summons. His eyes sought those of the A.C. 'T-the sketches, they would be quite accurate?' he inquired.

'Quite.' The police chief's eyes rested on him, levelly. There was anticipation in the glance.

'Ah! *T-then the m-murderer made two mistakes,*' the professor said, gently. The A.C's head nodded slightly, very slightly as though he followed the unspoken argument.

'The murderer!' The ejaculation came from three of the Dilettantes simultaneously. 'Then —'

'Oh, y-yes. It w-was m-murder.'

'An opinion,' the chairman said. 'From a sketch?'

'*W-why is the weapon lying near the dead man's right hand?*' The professor spoke mildly and very gently. A slight smile played round the A.C.'s eyes.

The pathologist sniffed a little. 'The man's reflexes would jerk it from his hand after the shot, and it would fall, naturally.'

'*W-why would a man who is left-handed shoot h-himself w-with a g-gun held in h-his r-right hand?*' The question came softly from the professor.

'Left-handed!' The chairman ejaculated. The professor chuckled, and it seemed strange coming from him. 'B-but y-yes,' he said. 'Look at the sketches. The bedside table is on the left of the bed. On the desk, t-the b-blotting-pad is to the right, so that there is space for the ink-pots and the pens and the paper rack on the left. The desk is placed so that the light from the window falls on t-the right s-side, w-which is w-where a man sitting left-handed would want it.' He addressed the chairman. 'Sir Noël, you are s-sitting at y-your desk, in which t-there are d-drawers. You refer to papers v-very often. On w-which side is t-the drawer in w-which y-you keep your references?'

The chairman's left hand moved involuntarily to the front of the table.

'So!' The professor pointed to it. 'But the drawer in which Banting kept t-the w-wallet w-which Mary t-the

maid says held h-his papers w-was on t-the right —
w-where a left-handed man, pen in hand w-would keep it.
T-the m-murderer forgets t-that Banting was left-handed.
He drops t-the gun on the wrong side. But you cannot
escape the inevitability of logical reasoning.'

'And the second mistake?'

'The man Banting goes upstairs t-to his room. He
unlocks t-the door and enters. He is carrying t-the key —
how? W-with h-his left hand. B-but he p-places t-the key
on the *right-hand* side of the desk. Lastly, why s-should
a man force his drawer when h-he h-has a key to it?' The
professor peered up at the A.C. from under his shock of
unruly hair. He fingered the high collar of his old-fashioned 'dicky.' Slowly, he produced a box and took from it
a pinch of snuff between his short, stubby fingers, brushing off the particles of dust which dropped on to the
shining lapel of his ancient jacket. 'You said, Sir Edward
that your inspector called to the room the old waiter and
put to h-him a question. A-afterwards he asked for t-the
M-murder Squad.' He giggled, delightedly. 'I will tell you
the question. The inspector asked how he laid the table for
Banting. Yes?'

The A.C. nodded, 'Congratulations, Professor, on your
perspicuity,' he said.

'Yet — you are still not sure, Edward?' the chairman
remonstrated.

'There is the possible interposition of coincidence. A
man, his mental balance upset by a decision to take his
own life, may break the habit of a lifetime. As for the forced
drawer, there were no keys in the pockets of Banting's suit.
We found them in the trousers pocket of an evening suit
which Banting had not worn for a fortnight. He may have
thought he had lost his keys — and so forced the drawer.
We have to be sure, you know. And, you will remember the

room was locked and, except for Banting, was empty — and there were only two minutes since the shot.'

Mr. James, who was the pathologist, leaned forward. 'The head wound, Edward? You have a medical report?'

'Yes.' The A.C. consulted again his notes. 'There was some tearing of the skin at the entrance, and an exit wound at the back of the head.'

'Any blackening of the skin, and powder marks?'

'Blackening — no. A little marking, not a great deal.'

'Then, I must agree with the professor.' He responded to the inquiring looks of the Dilettantes. 'If a discharge occurs at a distance of 6 to 12 inches no tearing of the skin takes place and the entrance wound is seen as a rounded hole with a bruised margin and surrounded with a zone of blackening, as well as impacted particles of powder. The powder marks disperse as the distance increases, until at two or three feet there may be little sign of powder. I should say, therefore, that the shot was fired from a distance of three feet or so, Edward?'

The A.C. acknowledged. 'I accept the theory of murder. We are inclined to it. But tell me, who is the murderer and where is he — or rather what happened to him. He could not have escaped into the corridor. Mary would have seen him. He did not escape into the street.'

'The barrel-organ men?' asked James.

'They were questioned, and saw nobody leave the house. They heard the shot when they were practically opposite the house, but thought something big had dropped in the basement and took no notice of it.'

'This lounge,' the professor said. 'D-describe it for me.'

'It is fairly large, with a door leading to a porch and to the front door. There's a large window, and a fireplace. It is really a hall. At the far end a door leads to the domestic quarters where a staircase goes down to the basement kitchen, and a servants' staircase upstairs.' He grinned at the look which appeared on the faces in front of him. 'Oh, no, nobody went down that way after the shooting; they would have to pass Mary, who was practically on top of it round the corner from which she peered.'

'Well, Edward, I see no solution,' Sir Noël said, 'any more than you do.'

The professor cleared his throat. The company turned to him. He fingered his tie, and then waggled a finger at them as though at students during a lecture. 'This is an impossible situation,' he said. 'And logic does not admit that the impossible can happen. Logic deals s-systematically with the principles which regulate valid thought, that is thought of which the c-conclusions are justified by the facts given; it enables us to judge whether any given evidence is sufficient to prove a given statement, and to perceive what additional statements can justifiably be inferred from any given statements. It has been called the science of proof and the study of the general conditions of valid inference.

'One assumption to logical reasoning is the Law of Contradiction. I will illustrate it from our present argument. This is how it works:

Murder is committed in a locked bedroom.

There is no murderer in the room.

Therefore the murderer has escaped.

'B-but if it can be proved beyond argument that the murderer could not possibly have escaped from the room, as Sir Edward has proved here, then you are left with the contradiction:

Murder has been committed in a locked bedroom.

The murderer has been unable to escape.

Therefore the murderer is still in the locked room.

'From that syllogism, gentlemen, there is no p-possible extrication. So the murderer of Banting was in the locked room all the time. That you d-did not see him does not eliminate him from the room —'

'But hang it all, Professor, people crowded into the room when the door was opened. One of them must have seen him —'

'Go on, Professor,' the A.C. said. 'You interest me greatly.'

'I can see him, white-faced, terror stricken, with the gun in his gloved hands. He had gone to the room to rob, at a safe time, while the guests were in the lounge with coffee. And then, unexpectedly Banting comes in and finds him. There is a crisis. He is to be assaulted by the angry Banting. He is at the desk, which he has been searching — for the papers missing from the wallet. He has seen the revolver and t-takes it out to threaten until he can pass Banting who is between him and the door. Banting moves towards him, and he fires. And he is in m-mortal peril. The shot has been heard. Already men are coming up the stairs. He can hear them. But he is quick-witted, and his wits are quickened even more by danger. And he escapes — by those wits.'

They stared at him with his eyes dancing in excitement beneath the grey shock of hair, and snuff particles gathering on his right lapel, which in his excitement he failed to brush off.

'But how, my dear man, how?' the chairman asked.

5

'THERE is only one way in which he could have escaped,' the professor went on after drinking a glass of wine. 'Only one way. *And I know that way, I, the logician.*'

'Tell us, there's a good fellow. Or rather, tell Sir Edward.'

'Tell you, ah no. T-that w-would be no m-mystery.' The spell and narrative broken, the professor lapsed into his slight stutter. 'I will show you. We will play the drama all over again.' He turned to the chairman. 'It would be permissible to use the service room for a little while, and to h-have the estimable waiter. H-he c-can be the Banting man.' He rang the bell. The waiter entered.

'Emile, we would like you, if you'll permit it, to help us in a little experiment.' the chairman said.

'Sirs.'

The professor opened the door of the service room. 'It is empty, as you see,' he said. He picked up the silver cigarette box from the dining-table, and carried it to the service room placing it on the serving-flap. He returned to the company. 'W-we are s-six,' he said, 'and all together. Emile, he will go into the service room and the door will be closed. He will lie down on the floor like Banting.' He demonstrated the lying himself.

'Ah, there is one important thing. The g-guests in the house had no suspicion that a man would die. You, my friends have. It is necessary that the rooms should be in darkness. When I turn off the lights, Sir Edward will count slowly up to ten. At ten, Emile will walk into the service-room. Sir Edward will count ten once more. And he will then clap his hands simulating a shot. And then you will rush into the service-room exactly as the guests did on that evening. And so we trap a murderer.'

The lights went out. At the call of ten they heard Emile walk to the door and enter the service-room. At the call of ten again the A.C. clapped his hands, and rushed into the service-room. With the exception of Emile on the floor, the room was empty. They walked back into the dining-room, and dismissed the waiter. They eyed the smiling professor.

'Y-you see,' he said, and pointed to the table.

On it was the silver cigarette box which had been placed on the ledge of the serving-room. The chairman stared.

'Who brought that out?' he asked and looked round the members. Each shook a negative head.

'T-the m-murderer of poor Emile escaped, you see, and he put back the box on the table,' the professor said.

The A.C. sat down. His face was grave. 'It was one of the eight,' he said. 'And yet, they were together. Tell me, Professor.'

'It h-had to b-be, Sir Edward. Logic, purely applied, can make no error. Because there were eight people in the lounge when Banting went upstairs, and after Banting was dead, d-does not mean there were eight there all the time. And because four men were in the room of Banting together, is not to assume that four men went in together. There was one who left the company before Banting. He slipped unostentatiously through the kitchen entrance and went up the servants' staircase to Banting's room. Mary would be in a bedroom on her duties. Banting surprised him and was shot. And the murderer was trapped. But he had the genius.

'As the alarmed guests hammered at the door, he stood quietly, his back to the wall at the side of the door. *When they unlocked it, threw it open and rushed in, he stepped from his hiding behind the door and joined them* — as I did just now. The others *expected* him to be with them in the room and they were sure he came with them.'

'Masterly,' the chairman said, and there was a chorus of agreement. The professor waved a hand. 'It i-is n-nothing,' he said. 'Logic — it is irrefutable.'

'Which?' The A.C. asked the question, he seemed to be speaking to himself.

'B-but t-there can be only one,' the professor said. 'He did not know that Banting was left-handed. Who would that be, but one who had not been long enough in the company to know it. T-there w-was one, you said, w-who h-had been there only a day or two.'

'Norris,' the A.C. said; and went to telephone.

6

FOUR meetings of the Dilettantes sped their destined course before there developed any problem of mundane interest. That is not to say that the distinguished members had not, in the meantime, pursued their infinite scholarship. Two sessions had been united in an excursus into philosophy, and the confusion into which the modern trend of thought has thrown it. But you are hardly likely to be excited in the modern scepticism which has narrowed and limited the scope of the traditional philosophy of Lindsay; or in the problem of whether the truth of philosophy is, as Bergson has asserted, that 'intuition' is the means by which the true nature of reality as a continuous flow is realized; or whether it is by means of reason that men have believed information about the universe is to be obtained; or, thirdly, whether the truth lies in pragmatism — that reason functions only to serve our purpose, and the so-called truths at which it arrives are, in fact, only those which it suits us to believe. Suffice it to say that the argument was waged on the high academic standard natural to the Dilettantes, with the case for Reason, pure and unadulterated, expounded by the professor — as was to be expected from a logician.

It was at the second of the September gatherings that Mr. Norman Charles, the psychiatrist, mentioned an incident which had provided the popular Press with a front page sensation. No topic for discussion had been arranged for the evening, and desultory conversation was proceeding over the vintage port of 1927 brought by the chairman from his own cellar — a vintage which Portugal has not equalled since that happy year.

Charles had poked his cigar in the direction of Allen. 'That Bath case is an extraordinary affair, is it not, Sir Edward?' he suggested. 'I should have liked the opportunity to examine the mind of a man who suddenly and so unaccountably lapses from a life of rectitude into a crazy act of criminality.'

'Oh, I don't know,' Sir Noël Maurice postulated from the chair. 'I should say simply a case of human greed, a growing failing in society these days.'

The professor peered from beneath his shock of greying hair, glancing quickly from one to the other of the two men. 'I d-do n-not read the n-newspapers,' he announced. 'W-what w-would it be t-that has h-happened?'

The chairman caught the A.C.'s eye. 'Well, Edward?' he queried. 'It may precipitate us into an instructive study of the vagaries of the human mind.' He laughed. 'I suspect that to be the reason for Charles raising it.'

The Assistant Commissioner (Crime) of Scotland Yard nodded. 'It'll be the agenda for the evening,' he agreed. He swallowed a sip of port — 'I hope you have more of this vintage, Noël' — and drew on his cigar.

'Well, it's rather a simple case,' he began. 'The two people concerned are John Benton, and his partner. Benton was 68 years of age. He had lived all his life in Bath where he occupied a prominent position as a citizen and tradesman. He was a jeweller, head of the firm of J. Benton

& Co., which he had himself founded twenty years ago. The firm had a good reputation not only in Bath, but throughout the county, most of the county families entrusting him with their jewellery for cleaning, re-setting and so on. As many of the families have London residences, he had a considerable clientele here as well.'

The A.C. paused to flip the ash from his cigar and to pull it up to a red glow. Then he continued: 'Benton was a man of leisurely habits. He took his time over repairs — he was a craftsman, by the way — and he was old-fashioned in a business sense; he preferred sitting in his shop waiting for customers to come rather than go after business. Two years ago he took into partnership a young man named Thomas Derja, who had been twelve months with another firm of jewellers in the city, and was well regarded in the trade. Derja had saved £2,000 and with it bought a small share in the firm.

'Now, he was as active in business as Benton was somnambulistic. He set out to attract business. He made appointments with members of wealthy families in the district and discussed with them their jewellery, suggesting the modernizing of the settings, thereby adding to the value. He also noted Society notifications of engagements, births and so on, and in this manner sold jewelled celebrations. The effect of all this was a substantial increase in the firm's revenue which, up to Derja's coming had been declining, a natural effect of taxation and death duties on the old wealthy families.'

At this stage of the story the chairman held up a hand to interrupt. 'I suggest we give Edward a breathing space while we refill our glasses,' he said. 'During that time we can digest the details he has given us.' Some five minutes were thus occupied in sampling quietly the vintage port. Then, refreshed and fortified, the A.C. resumed.

'You will appreciate,' he said, 'that what I have told you is the result of intensive inquiries by Scotland Yard officers — from townspeople and the assistants in Benton & Co. The latter are emphatic in their view that Derja was a valuable acquisition to the firm. In appearance he is a slim, dark young man of 36 with an attractive personality and considerable appeal to women. Most of his sales were to members of the fair sex.

'About twelve months ago he was seized with another business brain-wave. It is common knowledge that quite a few of the older county families are in considerably reduced financial circumstances, particularly where it is obvious that they will in the near future have to consider finding death duties. Derja worked on this, along singularly enticing lines. Old Benton knew just what jewellery such people had, because he had been cleaning and preserving it for years, gems that had been bought by them in their more opulent days — and he knew their present indigence. Derja, armed with his partner's knowledge, and with his authority, approached them and suggested they should convert their more extravagant jewellery into cash. To their horrified reaction that they would never have it known that they were compelled to sell their jewels, he assured them there would be no question of any publicity; such sales would be carried out by the firm by private treaty, and the name of the seller would not be revealed; the goods would be the property of a lady — or gentleman.'

'It worked. Opportunities for wearing elaborate diamond ornaments these days are restricted; in twelve months Derja negotiated sales amounting to some £80,000 on which the firm drew a commission of ten per cent. All this is square and above board; the sales, and commission, are entered in the firm's private sales book; and the amounts of commission are in the ledgers.'

7

THE company was following the A.C.'s narration with absorbed interest. The professor had been leaning forward, his right elbow on the table supporting his forearm, the hand of which was cupping his chin. Now and then he relaxed his attitude to take copious pinches of snuff, the evidence of which was spattered on the lapel of his ancient jacket; but even so he still peered at the speaker through the thick lenses of his spectacles.

Charles's eyes were staring past the speaker; he seemed pre-occupied as though, as a psychiatrist, he was probing into the personalities of the men the A.C. was describing. The police chief waited, the lingers of his right hand twisting the black silk ribbon of his monocle; he was apparently assembling in his mind the points of the investigation and how best to present them. Presently, he came to a decision and dropped his monocle to the full length of its ribbon.

'It was one of these sales that brought tragedy and police investigations,' he said. Mr. Derja had for disposal a £5,000 necklace belonging to a Mrs. Helen Mildenhurst, an elderly woman, and an invalid. She said she saw no likelihood of ever again going into those circles and occasions where £5,000 necklaces are worn, and might as well have the money. The firm put the transaction through, selling the necklace to Mr. Isaac Bonheimer. You probably know he can well afford it; and the problem of occasions for wearing it would not arise with Mrs. B, who once sold cockles from a stall in the East End of London; she will probably wear it for breakfast!

'The necklace was to be handed over last Tuesday, and the partners agreed to deliver it together. It is important now to mark the events of the day. Mr. Benton had spent the previous day refurbishing the necklace. At 8.25 o'clock

Mr. Derja called at the shop for his partner. Benton had arrived a minute or two earlier. Then Mr. Benton went to the safe and took out the necklace in its case and placed it in an inside pocket of his jacket. The pair then took a taxi to the station at 8.30 and subsequently boarded the 9.18 train to London. They had seats in the Pullman car — two single chairs facing each other across a table. The car was half filled. Full breakfasts were being served which Mr. Derja says neither of them wanted, having had a snack meal at their homes.

'But at Swindon Mr. Benton, his partner says, stated that he felt a little peckish. As luck would have it a trolley selling fruit and other things stopped opposite the Pullman. Derja let down the window and bought a packet of wrapped ham sandwiches. Now I will give you Mr. Derja's account of the subsequent happenings. He said: 'After the train had restarted we ordered two cups of coffee. I asked the steward for a knife with which to cut the two rounds of sandwiches, but he was a bit annoyed at our buying food off the platform and didn't bring one. So I borrowed Mr. Benton's knife and cut a sandwich in half. I took one piece and Mr. Benton the other. We drank some of the coffee and started to eat. Next thing I knew was that Mr. Benton gasped, gave a kind of gurgle and slipped down half under the table. Then someone said he was dead.'

The pathologist broke in. 'He had not complained of feeling unwell?'

'No. He appeared in his usual health.'

'And spirits?'

'We made exhaustive inquiries of his wife and the staff at the shop. The reply was that he was his usual self, and had been pleased at the deal which the firm was putting through.'

The A.C. looked inquiringly at Charles, but the pathologist nodded his satisfaction; and Sir Edward continued. 'At this point there was for us a fortuitous interruption. In the car was a Mr. William Archer, a private investigator, but who had served twenty years with the Bath C.I.D. He helped to extricate Mr. Benton from underneath the seat, and lay him along the centre corridor of the Pullman coach. Then, as he explained later, he did not like the look of him. He bent over him, saw that his eyes were open and staring, with the pupils dilated. He felt the skin at the back of the neck and found it to be cold. He called the chief steward, had a few words with him, and as a result the car was cleared of passengers and the doors at each end locked. At Reading the train was slowed to a near-stop and the guard threw a note in front of a porter. When the train reached London we were waiting.'

He laughed. 'Give me some more of that excellent port, Noël,' he said to the chairman. 'It's dry work talking.' For a few moments he relaxed in his chair; and then continued:

'In the meantime a startling development occurred. Up to then Mr. Derja had assumed that his partner had died from a heart attack. Mr. Archer undeceived him — unwittingly. He mentioned poison. Whereupon Mr. Derja shrieked. 'From poison?' he said. 'Do you mean he's taken — my God, the diamonds'. He rushed over to the body, but was pulled back by Archer, and warned not to touch Mr. Benton. It was then that he told the story of the diamonds. Mr. Archer realized that if there were diamonds they had better be in safe keeping. He went to Benton and feeling inside his breast pocket extracted the case. He opened it and revealed the necklace. Mr. Derja wiped perspiration from his brow. Archer held up the case for him to see. 'Are these the diamonds?' he asked.

'Now an extraordinary thing occurred; and I will give it to you as Mr. Archer told us. He said:

'As I held up the case and asked Mr. Derja said 'Yes . . . I was afraid . . .' Then he stopped. A flash had come from the necklace as the lights in the car struck it. Derja called out 'What was that?' 'What was what?' I asked. 'Please let me see those diamonds,' he said. I passed them over and he pulled a jeweller's eyepiece from a pocket and bent over the case. In a minute he straightened up. He was breathing heavily, and his hands were open and shutting. 'Sir,' he said. 'Sir, something has happened. This . . . and . . . this . . .' he pointed to some of the diamonds . . . 'are not diamonds at all. They are false. They are prisms. I knew it when the stones flashed in the light. The diamond gives a blue colour, not prism colours. They are faked. So he commits suicide . . . he is a faker.'

'That is the story we heard when Superintendent Jones and our Inspector met the train on arrival in London.'

8

THERE was a little stir among the listening Dilettantes — like a breeze rustling leaves. The A.C. had been speaking quietly and undemonstratively, but he had a flair for the dramatic which the tranquillity of his delivery accentuated rather than diminished. Some great actors have it; Eleanora Duse was more moving in repose than in her histrionics; the declamations of Olivier are never so effective as were the quiet modulations of Martin-Harvey or Forbes-Robertson.

The silence which followed the stir was broken by the chairman. 'It must have been quite a moment,' he said. 'On the stage it would be immense. But why should Derja jump to the conclusion that his partner was a faker and had committed suicide. Could not the stones have been there all the time?'

'The replacements might have been done by the original owner,' Purcell suggested. The A.C. smiled slightly and eyed them quizzically.

'Ah! That is the acme of the affair,' he said. 'When the sale was first mooted and Mr. Bonheimer contacted and interested, Derja took the necklace to London for Mr. and Mrs. Bonheimer to see. Mr. Bonheimer quite naturally wanted a valuation and the necklace was taken to a valuer accompanied by the principals and Derja. The firm was Alpen & Moore, pretty well-known people. After a thorough examination they gave the Bonheimers a written valuation for; £5,000, 'or more'. A copy was also given to Derja. That was on Friday of last week. On that Bonheimer agreed to buy, the deal to be carried through on Tuesday.'

'Well, dash it, Edward, where's the acme about that?' the chairman asked. 'Good lord, I should have wanted an opinion on the thing other than that of an old woman and Derja.'

The A.C. chuckled. 'Don't be impatient, Noël, I haven't touched the summit, yet. On Tuesday morning a letter arrived at Bentons from Bonheimer. The post there is delivered at 7 o'clock. The letter was waiting for him when he entered the shop at 8.25. It asked that Benton when he reached London with the necklace should go straight to the offices of a Hatton Garden firm for a valuation for insurance purposes. Mr. Bonheimer would meet him there.'

'Oh!' The exclamation came from all five listeners.

'Quite so!' Sir Edward looked gratified at the reception accorded his dramatic vertex. 'The necklace had been interfered with — there is no doubt about that and our own jewel expert confirmed it — and there is no doubt the interference would have been spotted immediately by the Garden firm — and the fraud exposed.'

'No blessed wonder he committed suicide,' Purcell said. 'He was booked for gaol.'

'Why on earth did Benton go through with it when he knew the certain outcome?'

'What could he do?' the A.C. protested. 'Had he not gone, Derja would on his own. And perhaps he hoped for some miracle: a casual examination, formally, from the Garden firm's knowledge of his own reputation.'

'Did he say anything about the letter?

'Oh, yes, indeed. According to Derja he was very upset and angry. Said there was no reason for another valuation; it was unheard of, and a reflection on his reputation and on the valuers who had already certified it.'

'Very significant,' Purcell said. 'What it comes to is that secure in the knowledge that a valuation had been made, and that Bonheimer had bought the necklace, Benton sets to work, extracts the more valuable stones and replaces them. Bonheimer would never have known the difference. Then when the letter arrives, he starts out with a forlorn hope of by-passing the new valuation, sees in the train the impossibility — and commits suicide?'

'That is the suggestion,' the A.C. agreed.

'Why did Bonheimer want the second valuation, if he was satisfied with the first one — and agreed on the price?'

The A.C. chuckled: it was more grim than humorous. 'Because of two words — just two words which brought, unwittingly, death.' He looked at Charles. 'Come, Norman, you're a psychiatrist. What is the answer?' Charles ruffled his brows, eyeing the police chief. 'No,' he said at last. 'I don't get it.'

'No? The original valuation said £5,000 or more. The instincts of Mr. Bonheimer rose to the 'or more'. He wanted to insure the necklace for more than the £5,000 he was paying for it. He hoped the second valuation would give a figure to the 'more!' We asked him — and got that reply.'

A ripple of laughter greeted the explanation: to be broken by the pathologist. 'What does Derja have to say about it?'

'A great deal. The sale, of course, is off, and he is left with a necklace worth far less than was paid for it. He says that since Benton did the fiddling, he will insist that reparation of the amount is made to the firm from Benton's personal finances. But that is not the extent of his worries — by long chalks.'

The professor had not spoken throughout the whole telling. Now he suddenly looked up at the A.C.

'Q-quite so. T-there h-had been, of course, o-other sales,' he said gravely. 'And if in o-one, w-why not in others?

The A.C. inclined his head in affirmation. 'So far we have inspected three articles,' he said. 'All have been ravished. In two cases diamonds of similar size but of inferior quality, had been substituted in almost an entire bracelet. It seems likely that many thousands of pounds will have to be paid back to the purchasers, and in addition the articles, themselves, are now of minor value.'

'What did he do with the stones he extracted?'

The A.C. spread his hands. 'We do not know. The shop and his home have been combed through — Derja insisted on that. We even went through the shop's stock with a jewellery expert, in case he might have turned them into rings, brooches, or such-like. You know that diamonds can be easily identified by their carat weight and cutting. He had not, so far as we can discover, sold any stones, or sent any away.'

'Cyanide, I see,' James, the pathologist said with interest in his voice. 'How did he take it — in the coffee I suppose?'

'Not in the coffee. There was no trace of cyanide in his cup, nor in Derja's. According to the post-mortem it was mixed with the food.'

'With food? That's an odd circumstance. In the sandwich? Do you think it might have been an accident?'

The A.C. shook his head. 'Quite impossible. Remember Derja's description of events: 'I cut a sandwich in half. I took one piece, Mr. Benton the other.' Benton's was half-eaten, Derja's part was also half-eaten: we have both the remains, with the cups and saucers and knife that were on the table.'

The professor tapped on the table for silence and made his second contribution of the evening: 'At w-what h-hour do the s-shops open in Bath, Sir Edward?' he asked.

'Time? — Let me see. Ah! we had to wait until 9 o'clock.'

9

'WELL, there you are. That is the whole of the tragic story,' the A.C. concluded. 'Criminologically, it is closed so far as we at the Yard are concerned. The only interest it has for me is in the man himself. What psychological act of sabotage came over him that could lead him to destroy his life and ruin the business he had built up over twenty years?'

'Money — and more money, Edward,' the chairman said.

'I don't think so, Noël.' The A.C. shook his head emphatically. 'Remember he was 68 and had quite a tidy fortune. He was a man of simple tastes and the money he possessed would have lasted him all his life; and he had no children to whom to leave it. Actually, he was living well below his income over the past two or three years and his capital was mounting. I don't think money was the reason. Does a man destroy wantonly for a pittance the monument to his ability and integrity?'

'Quite a number of thousands is hardly a pittance, Edward,' the chairman interposed. 'And 'each man kills the thing he loves' — Oscar Wilde, isn't it?'

'Poetic fancy. The reason I have told the story at such length is that I thought it might provide a topic for us to-night.' He looked across at Norman Charles. 'Come, Norman, you are a psychiatrist, and the professor has philosophy and reason. What do you suggest overtook him?'

Charles rubbed a hand over his chin. 'A psychiatrist works from the reactions of a living person, not a dead one, Edward. It is more in the line of psychology' — he nodded across at the professor — 'but I'll have a shot.' He thought for a moment or two. 'Freud posited an 'unconscious' inaccessible by ordinary methods of observation, but with a strong life of its own which continually affects the conduct of the individual. His teaching was on a theory that continual mental conflicts are going on in all minds below the threshold of consciousness, their object being to keep away from observation the ideas and wishes which are abhorrent to conscience. Well, something occurs, most frequently perhaps in late life, when that mental conflict is lost, and it comes out in physical conduct. It was there all the time below the level of consciousness, but held in check. A circumstance, quite trivial or simple, can bring it out — a shock, a disagreement, a sudden aversion to someone or something. What did it to Benton we are not likely now to know. Repression is one likely cause, and with repressions sexual reasons are general. That may have been the case with Benton. He was a married man, but had never had any family. Perhaps he had wanted children, and the thought that he had no one to follow him in his business worked on him, hidden, until it suddenly exploded. Since jewels were his love his mental surrender to conscience turned in their direction.'

James broke in: 'Pathologically, it is possible to link sexual influences with such a case in another way,' he said. 'Those mental changes which so often affect women at the climacteric also occur in men between the ages of 55 and 65. It can be delayed until even later and then the results are frequently much more serious. Usually, such a change leads to melancholia. It could however affect a man's code of morality. But — well, the professor is more versed in the subject and in reasoning; and he has been very quiet tonight. Well, Professor?'

Dr. Stubbs took a copious pinch of snuff from his silver box. Slowly and deliberately he brushed away the dust left from it from his waistcoat before he raised his goblin-like head, and turned his thick lenses on the A.C. and spoke:

'W-why d-did Mr. Benton h-have cyanide w-with him on t-the train?' he asked, mildly.

They stared at him. The A.C. replied:

'I can't say why he had cyanide. But if he intended suicide, then some poison was necessary. And cyanide is easily obtained.'

'Q-quite!' A shadow which might have been a smile crossed the professor's face. He waved a hand. 'Freud!' he said. 'He has been discarded for years. He based his theories on inherited instincts, tendencies and environment. W-what h-have h-his t-theories to do with Mr. Benton and w-with t-the age of 68? Phooey! T-there are one or t-two t-things I w-would like to know. T-the shop of Mr. Benton, it is a lock-up?'

The A.C. nodded.

'And t-there are t-two partners — t-they have k-keys: and who else?'

'The chief assistant.'

'And t-the setting of jewels, and repairs and t-the fashioning of jewellery, it w-was done b-by Mr. Benton himself?'

'Always. Derja was, in plain terms, a salesman.'

'But a trained jeweller.'

'Yes. He had spent seven years' apprenticeship.'

'So. It is g-good.' The professor settled himself in his chair, thought for a moment and looked round the table. 'W-we t-talked earlier this evening about philosophy,' he said. 'Philosophy and p-psychology are allied sciences; indeed for a generation they w-were r-regarded as one until t-the nineteenth century, in fact. But w-without one other science, they are useless — without the science of reasoning. Yes?' His spectacles, like gig-lamps, roved round the table, and noted the agreeing inclination of five heads. 'And reasoning is the Science of Logic. I, Marcus Stubbs, t-tell y-you t-this. Also, I t-tell you t-that I have listened t-to the story so admirably t-told by Sir Edward' — he bowed in the direction of the A.C. — 'listened most earnestly, and I h-have h-heard only t-that which my reasoning will not accept. Gentlemen, t-the w-whole of this s-story is so abhorrent a lie as t-to m-make me t-tremble in anger.'

A sharp intake of breath sounded round the table. The chairman found his voice.

'Come, come, Professor!' he chided.

'Logic is i-irrefutable. I t-tell y-you s-so.' The man in the passion of his denunciation was spluttering in a hesitating stammer at almost every word. 'T-there is n-no l-logic or r-reason here. B-but I must b-be c-calm. Reason h-has no p-passion. It is suggested t-that sexual re-repression sent Mr. Benton to crime. Nonsense! He is a m-man m-married more than forty years. D-do you t-think with seriousness that a desire to have had a child and an heir to his possessions would break out after forty years? Or before it? W-what h-have we here? A man, upright and courageous, who b-built up a b-business over twenty years and then destroys it for something — money and diamonds — of which he had no need. W-what reasoning is that?

'L-let us apply t-the principles of correct and logical thought. Sir Edward, I asked you w-why Mr. Benton h-had cyanide on t-the t-train. You replied that if he intended t-to commit suicide t-then some poison was necessary. There, indeed, is pragmatism — a reasoning only to serve our purposes, to convince us what we want to believe. Let us s-study t-the facts. On Monday night the necklace is a safely s-sold article, valued, approved, and ready for delivery to the customer. On T-Tuesday morning at 8.25 Mr. Benton enters his shop. A minute later Mr. Derja joins him. They were never apart from that moment. The letter f-from Mr. Bonheimer asking for the second valuation was in the shop letter-box, and it was o-opened and r-read. Mr. Benton is annoyed, indeed angry. There was no reason for another valuation, he s-said. B-but, he did n-not p-panic. He d-did n-not say: 'To hell with the man. I will not be so treated. Telephone him that the deal is off. We will sell elsewhere.' Thus, gentlemen, the necklace could go back into the safe, and be restored in safety. After all, Mr. Benton is the senior partner, t-the boss. But w-what does he do? He g-goes to London — to certain exposure; and in t-the t-train it is s-said he commits suicide.

'Gentlemen, I ask Sir Edward and you: *Why h-had Mr. Benton cyanide w-with him on the t-train. And where did he g-get it?* He d-did not w-want it on Monday night; there was no likelihood then of discovery of the fraud. He did not want it until 8.25 on Tuesday morning — until he opened the Bonheimer letter and learned of the new valu-ation, and what it would mean to h-him. The shops in Bath do not open until 9 o'clock. At 8.30 o'clock he was in a taxi with Mr. Derja, at 9 o'clock he was on the station. And he and Derja w-were together all the t-time. And yet he h-had cyanide? Is t-that sound r-reasoning, g-gentlemen?'

'Is it?' he demanded again; and leaned back in his chair. His eyes, seen big through the thick lenses, turned on the A.C., searching the face of the police chief. Slowly, he took another pinch of snuff, and straightened the 'dicky' inside his vest. The Dilettantes were listening in strained attitudes, and waiting impatiently. The profes-sor started again.

'B-but s-suppose Mr. Benton had k-known n-nothing of the re-replacements in the necklace, he w-would have been angry at the d-demand for another valuation — as, indeed, he was. B-but t-that is all. It w-would n-not really matter to h-him. The necklace, he knows, is genuine. T-then, gentlemen, t-there is nothing inconsistent with his journey to London.'

'Except that he committed suicide, Professor,' the chairman pointed out.

'Except t-that he d-died, Sir Noël.'

Sir Edward Allen spoke for the first time since the professor had started. 'Go on, Professor,' he said: and his voice was very low.

'Then, let us proceed w-with further s-supposition,' the logician went on. 'Let us s-suppose there is someone who does know the necklace is false and who, when the discovery is made by the new valuation is in that same p-peril of p-prison, *unless he c-can s-shift the b-blame —* for t-that and the other falsifications. And s-suppose in t-the t-train, in perfect security as it appeared, he, is ready for such emergency which was always p-possible, he — *shifts the blame.*'

'We would require very strong presumptive evidence, Professor,' the A.C. warned.

'T-the n-necklace, Sir Edward. It s-shall provide it. Mr. Benton is dead in t-the c-car. Mr. Archer mentions poison. And Derja wails: 'My God, the diamonds' and w-when the c-case is re-recovered from Mr. Benton's pocket said: 'I was afraid —'' The professor looked round. 'Afraid of w-what? He h-had b-been with Mr. Benton all t-the t-time. W-what did he t-think could have h-happened to the diamonds. W-where *should* t-they b-be but in his p-partner's pocket? The mind should reason. Sir Edward, not as it wants, or is induced by set clues to believe, but dispassionately.'

The professor sniffed from the inevitable snuff box. The company waited. 'Then, Mr. Archer opens t-the c-case and holds it up. The n-necklace catches the light. 'Those are not the diamonds,' Derja says. 'I knew it when the prisms flashed'.' The professor laughed aloud, and the laugh had a mocking sarcasm in it. 'From a single glint of light on a row of flashing diamonds he s-sees only t-the primary colours from t-two or t-three prisms! Eyesight the most remarkable. But — *if he k-knew t-that there must be prism colours —*' The professor spread out his hands, short and stubby with the cuticles of the index fingers stained with his snuff.

Sir Edward Allen leant forward. 'It is a clever and ingenious hypothesis, Professor,' he admitted. 'And a circumstantial one. I would think it well worth probing, except that it is negatived by one solid and undeniable *fact*: Benton is dead, and Derja is alive. And they ate from the same sandwich, with the undigested remains of which in Benton the poison that killed him was mixed.'

The Dilettantes sat silent. Their eyes turned to the figure of the little professor. He was tapping on his knees, and his gaze was centred on the A.C. They did not shift when he spoke:

'Who purchased t-the sandwiches, Sir Edward? Mr. Benton was peckish. Derja could h-have ordered from t-the s-steward of the car — as he did the c-coffee. Roll and cheese, even s-sandwiches. But then, they would have come on plates — one for each customer, and Mr. Benton would have taken his, and Derja his. But no, Derja buys a packet from a station trolley. He opens it. He borrows Mr. Benton's k-knife and presently, after they have drunk s-some c-coffee, he cuts a sandwich in two and gives one half to Mr. Benton, and starts on t-the other h-half himself.'

'Quite so,' the A.C. said: and he spoke pointedly. The professor ignored the remark — and the tone. 'Derja,' he said. 'It is an odd name. Malayan, yes?'

The A.C. nodded.

'P-perhaps from Kelentan, in the north?'

'Yes. He is a Kelentan. He has been in England for ten years.'

'You do not k-know Malaya, Sir Edward?'

'I have never been there.'

'A curious race, the Malayans.' The professor lapsed into reminiscence. 'I s-spent a y-year among them, s-studying t-the philosophy of the people. It d-differs so g-greatly from the philosophical outlook of the West. T-they are a fatalistic people, and —'

The A.C. shifted in his chair impatiently, and a quiet cough came from one or two of the other listeners. The professor went on, unmoved:

'In Kelentan t-they h-have an unpleasant w-way of d-dining a guest. The h-host, sharing a meal divides a water-melon in half w-with a k-knife. But the under-side of the k-knife has been smeared with honey w-with w-which has been mixed poison. He himself eats only t-that p-part of the melon on the c-clean side of the k-knife. The guest bites the edge of t-the other h-half which h-has taken from the blade the smeared poison. The poison is, of c-course, only on t-the edge of t-the melon, and t-the k-knife by the cutting is w-wiped clean of the p-poison. The remainder of the bitten piece of melon is without trace of poison. *And the poison thus used in Malaya is always cyanide.*'

The little man ignored the startled gasp that came from the men round the table.

'It w-would w-work equally w-well with a sandwich in the hands of a Malayan,' he said. 'T-the poison, p-prepared and ready say in a t-tube, squeezed under t-the screen of a t-table along one side of the k-knife-blade, and the sandwich then c-cut and the half with the poisoned edge, pushed across to t-the victim.'

He now spoke softly — as though communing with himself.

'The pocket-knife, drawn th-through t-the sandwich. It must retain cyanic traces — in t-the crick w-where it joins t-the handle; in t-the receptacle w-which shields t-the blade w-when c-closed. And, somewhere along the railway line is a t-tube, dropped through a window, or p-perhaps f-flushed d-down a lavatory I wonder —'

There was a slight commotion, and he looked up. The A.C. had started violently to his feet, met the eyes of the chairman, and received a nod of permission. He left the room very quickly.

Four Dilettantes sat quite still; no word was spoken. The professor poured out a glass of port, and held it in front of him.

'To the memory of an honest old man,' he said, and there was no stammer. *'Requiescat in pace.'*

10

As was the custom the port had circulated before the 'circle of the Sciences' — which is the sobriquet pinned on the Dilettantes by a witty and erudite Literary Critic — engaged in their fortnightly acromatics.

It was the meeting following the professor's masterly dialogism on the Bath train death. The Malayan, Derja, confronted with the reconstruction of the journey, had confessed and was waiting trial; and the club had extended to the professor its congratulations, to which the Assistant Commissioner of Scotland Yard added the appreciation of the commissioner himself.

'Have you recovered the stones removed from the various articles, Edward?' the chairman inquired.

Sir Edward frowned. 'No, we haven't,' he said. 'Derja maintains that he passed them over to the person who planned the depredations and, he says, compelled him by *force majeure* to carry them out.'

'The force being?' James asked.

'Something he had done in Malaya which, revealed, would result in his being deported back to Malaya. The person, I think, is imaginary. Derja was living far above his income.'

'Ah well,' Purcell said,

> 'Blood, like sacrificing Abel, cries
> Even from the tongueless caverns of the earth
> For justice.'

'Bolingbroke, I think.'

'Its cry was heard on this occasion,' Charles put in. 'But . . .' he hesitated. 'Are there really many unsolved murders, Sir Edward?'

The Assistant Commissioner turned his cigar between his fingers, and frowned a little. 'You touch a sensitive spot, there, Charles,' he said. 'If by unsolved you mean that the perpetrators are not known the answer is — very few. On the other hand taking unsolved as implying that justice has not been done, well, then, the total is higher. It is a question of evidence sufficient to convict. Failure to convict, and the murderer is free of peril —'

'Even if he stands at Marble Arch afterwards and says in the music-hall vernacular: 'I done it'?'

'Even then. Men we know to have committed murder are walking the streets to-day. They know that we know. You may remember some years ago the killing of a child in a coal-cellar at Bayswater. The man was always known to us. We watched him for years until he died; one slip and we could have hanged him. We are still watching three other men — and hoping. In other cases — well I admit we have been completely circumvented. The killing of a prostitute in a Soho back room is one instance.

'But' — he looked round and smiled —'the most perfect murder I've ever come across was carried out on the Italian Riviera, at San Remo to be precise. There was a circle of four dead men —'

'Four!' It came as a simultaneous cry from round the table.

'Four — and to this day we have not the slightest idea of the identity of the murderer — or why he murdered. It is of all deaths I have ever known the most bizarre and unaccountable.'

James, the pathologist, looked up; he had been searching his mind, his brows knitted. 'I do not recall reading of it, Edward,' he said.

'No. It didn't come to headlines in the British Press,' the A.C. said. 'Just a paragraph. It was primarily an Italian affair. The only reason we were concerned was because three of the dead were British — but of no account.'

'Bizarre, and unaccountable!' Purcell said. 'I think you ought to tell us, A.C.'

Sir Edward smiled, and the smile lit up his face. 'That is why I mentioned it,' he said. He looked across at the professor. 'I would like to hear your version of what *could* have happened.' He emptied his glass, and watched thoughtfully the chairman refill it: and began.

'The story really starts in London with three men. Their names were Thomas Morgan, Selwyn Lord and Timothy Vincent. Each was known to the police as a receiver of stolen property, mostly jewellery, though none had ever been convicted. It is normal police routine to keep unobtrusive observation on people such as these; and in due course it was noted that the three made regular trips to the Continent. It struck us as odd that when they thus travelled it was always on the same day and on the same train. Accordingly, when we found that one of them had taken tickets through a travel agency to San Remo on a day in July we put a detective-inspector from the Customs Squad on the train — the Blue Train, by the way, which has a through coach to San Remo.

'Very early on the officer noticed another odd circum-stance; though the three were well-known to each other, they acted as complete strangers on the train. They occu-pied each a first-class sleeper in a different coach. In the train bar they spent the evening drinking, but always apart and without acknowledgment; at meals in the restaurant they sat at different tables —'

'Probably wary in the presence of a detective-inspector,' James suggested.

'No.' The A.C. was emphatic. 'They did not know him from Adam. His duties and usual area were in London docks. At San Remo they left the train separately, each carrying a suitcase. Our man followed Morgan, to the Hotel Mediterranée, and saw him enter. And that was, believe it or not, the last he saw of any of them. Discreet inquiries at the hotel disclosed that no man of the name of Morgan, or any man of his description, had booked in; he had merely walked through the hotel and out of the garden entrance, which goes on to the sea promenade. A week later all three were once again in London.'

11

'THIS, Edward, promises to be absorbing,' the chairman interrupted. 'I suggest you keep us in healthy suspense for a minute or two while we fortify ourselves by filling our glasses, and lighting-up.' He pushed a box of cigars round the table, and followed it with the decanter. The *diver-tissement* completed, Sir Edward resumed his narrative.

'Where was I?' he said. 'Oh, yes, the three men were home again. Well we looked into the occasions on which they had been noted as crossing the Channel, and though the dates were not coincidental, they were sufficiently approximate to certain successful robberies as to suggest there was a definite connection with them as receivers. The next time they migrated all three were searched at the Customs both here and in France — the French people co-operating with us. To make doubly certain their belongings were gone through again in their sleepers on the train. We found nothing.

'During the succeeding nine months, two of the men went six times to the Riviera. The third went only four times, his absences being accounted for by the fact that his face had come into violent contact with a bicycle chain wielded by someone he declined to name.'

The A.C. paused to draw on his cigar. Not until he was satisfied with its evenness of glow did he continue. 'Now, on each and every visit they were searched.' He smiled, reminiscently. 'I do not suppose that anybody was ever subjected to so complete an examination as they were. We ripped open the insides of their suitcases, and X-rayed them. We searched their clothes, opened the seams, and the turn-ups of their trousers. We probed the soles and heels of their boots and the toe-caps. We even let them settle down in the security of their sleepers for the night, and then walked in and pulled the compartment to pieces. In doing so on one occasion we damaged beyond use a couple of hundred cigarettes bought at ship's prices. (They are a useful receptacle for hidden contraband). The result every time was negative; there was not a single article between them which was not legitimate.'

'Did they give any reason for the frequent visits?' Purcell asked.

'They did. Morgan said he was going to gamble at Monte Carlo — and he had a wad of French francs to show as capital; Lord, that he had a woman friend in Ospadalette; and Vincent that he had an interest in car deals with a San

Remo firm. We found out later that it was a remunerative business in stolen cars. Each and all denied any acquaintance with the others.

'At this point, when we had given up hope, there came a 'break.' An officer of the West End Division picked up on suspicion a little runt named Barker. He was known to be a 'drummer,' which is crooks' slang for a man who spots and tapes likely places to rob and passes on the information to receivers —'

'Receivers?' James looked surprised. 'Why to receivers?'

'Because most robberies worth while are organized by receivers, who choose the operatives and pay out a percentage on the proceeds. The officer toted Barker along to his lodgings and searched them — purely 'on spec.' And he found a choice collection of silver-ware, part proceeds of a burglary some weeks beforehand.'

Sir Edward ceased speaking and suddenly began to laugh: so heartily that tears dimmed his eyes. He dabbed them away with his handkerchief.

'Sorry,' he said, 'but I never fail to see the funny side whenever I think of it. It was the queerest 'break' the Yard ever had. Remember that the officer had not the slightest reason to apprehend Barker, except that vague and convenient excuse of 'loitering with intent.' Nor had he any reason to suspect that he would have stolen property in his room; he was not known to us as a thief. Well, Barker eyed the silver, which was under the bed-clothes, dumb-founded, and he jumped at once to the conclusion that he had been framed. He seemed to ruminate over the matter on the way to the police-station, for on arrival he asked to see a C.I.D. inspector and was taken to Inspector Lestrode. What he proposed to tell the inspector we never knew, because almost immediately an extraordinary incident occurred . . .'

Tantalizingly the A.C. chose this moment slowly to sip his port, rolling the vintage round his palate before swallowing, and enjoying the courteously masked suspense of his listeners. When it was wearing rather thin, the chairman intimated gently: 'An extraordinary incident, you said?' The A.C. chuckled.

'Yes. Barker had been planted in a chair at the side of the inspector's desk. Suddenly he pushed his chair violently backwards and shouted: 'So *HE* tried to shop me, did he, the — bastard. He said as how he'd put me inside.' The inspector looked at him in amazement. 'What are you havering about?' he asked, 'Who tried to shop you?' 'Don't give me that blarney. *HIM*,' Barker said, and pointed to a sheet of paper on the desk.

'Now it had so chanced (the A.C. went on) that that very morning our three men had been reported as having taken tickets for an Italian destination through an agency, and officers had been put on them to report their movements and actions. (Actually they left on the 11 o'clock train from Victoria). Lestrode had been writing out a report on the inquiries and had come to the end of one report sheets and written a continuation sentence at the head of another. When Barker was brought in he pushed the report aside and took a clean sheet for the man's expected statement. Barker, glancing round, read that sentence, all by itself on the report sheet. It said:

'Thomas Morgan telephoned at 8.30 o'clock'

and Barker jumped to the conclusion that he had been picked up because of the telephone call, and to the second conclusion that what Morgan had telephoned was to tell us what they would find in his (Barker's) room. Actually, had Lestrode completed the sentence it would have read —

'telephoned at 8.30 o'clock a Hampstead number, which was that of his own flat.'

'Lestrode, a wily old bird, merely asked: 'Why did he want to frame you?' and was told of a rumpus and recriminations over a slip-up between them, through which Morgan's sister was arrested. It doesn't matter here. What does matter is that Barker began whining and said: 'If I put you on to something you want about Morgan will you see me all right over the silver?' He was given the usual assurance that we would do the best we could for him, and then he talked.

'Morgan, Lord and Vincent, he said, were in a receivers' ring clearing stuff out of the country and working with an Italian receiver. They went out at regular intervals and met at the Villa Pinetta in the via della Visitagioni, in San Remo. The Italian, he said, was a Signor Giuseppe Martini, who was a highly respected individual in the town. They were due to go out again in the next day or so, and would be taking rubies, proceeds of a raid on Thorill Hall, in Cheshire, some months earlier.

'Lestrode brought him to us at the Yard, where he repeated the story at greater length. We thought it as well not to inquire how he knew all this. Then, we turned him loose — we should have done in any case. You see, examination showed that there was not a single one of his fingerprints on the silver, and we couldn't see how he could have stolen it, and cached it in his bed without leaving prints. He had, undoubtedly, been 'prepared' for a frame-up; but it wasn't by Morgan.'

12

'WELL, now we had something to act upon. A telephone call to Dover confirmed that the three men had sailed on the Cross-Channel boat, and that they had been Customed as usual and found clean. A Continental time table elicited that they would be decanted at San Remo at 12.30 midday next day, which would mean that any business to be done with the Italian would be after lunch.

'What we hoped to do was to walk in on the meeting —'

'Which you couldn't do, Edward,' the chairman said, 'not even by air line — at that time of night.'

'You underestimate us, Noël,' the A.C. retorted. 'We have a permanent emergency plane arrangement with a small charter company. We called him up and arranged for him to be waiting for Inspector Kenway and Sergeant Barratt at Gatwick and fly them to Imperia. All this happened as arranged, and the officers were at the police headquarters at midday. Inspector Lombarde was expecting them; and from them he heard the facts, and that we expected the three to be at the villa sometime which Kenway and Barratt worked out as not earlier than 2 o'clock. Accordingly, all three drove along the coast-road from Imperia to San Remo — and if you've never done it, you should; it's the most glorious panorama of coast I know.

'They parked the car in the Via Fiume, and walked round the corner to the Villa Pinetta. And there under a broiling sun with only a level-crossing hut as shelter, they began a watch at 1.30 o'clock. Nobody having visited the Villa by 3 o'clock Kenway decided on action. They would enter the Villa, confront Signor Martini and wait with him until his visitors walked unsuspectingly in. They rang the bell, which was answered by a red-headed Italian. His master, he said, was engaged. 'With three gentlemen, perhaps?'

Lombarde suggested, and received a *'Si, Signori.'* At that they pushed their way into what Kenway said was the most luxurious hall he'd ever seen: with marble floor, marble walls and marble pillars to hold up the ceiling; and a marble staircase. The floor was covered with Chinese rugs. Lombarde looked round, singled out a door and looked at the servant, who nodded. With Sergeant Barratt keeping guard in the hall, they crossed to the door. Lombarde tried the handle, and finding it unlocked, threw the door open.

'I don't know whether I will be able to make you visualize the utterly fantastic, the incredibly macabre scene which presented itself. Just give me a moment or so to remember how Kenway described it, later, in words and writing.'

Sir Edward leaned back in his chair, his eyes closed, and blew smoke rings from his cigar.

The professor had been so profoundly absorbed in the narrative that not once had he produced his snuff box — an omission which he now took the opportunity to remedy.

Presently the A.C. opened his eyes, drank half-a-glass of port, and leaned forward on the table, an attitude which seemed intended to impress upon his listeners what was to come.

'The room was a large one (he said) and magnificent with fittings and furniture you might expect to find in an Italian palace. The sideboard, chairs and foot-stools were of light-coloured wood, each decorated with hand-painted flowers in beautiful designs, and inset with panels in petit-point. And so was a grand piano set across a corner. A small circular table was also thus decorated, even to the legs. The room had two windows, and these, according to the Italian custom when the sun shines, were protected by Venetian window shutters pulled close. But the room was ablaze with light from a ten-light cut-glass chandelier.

'The table held four empty Florentine-glass tumblers, a bottle of Cinzano a quarter-full, a glass jug nearly empty of water, a box of Italian cigarettes, a table lighter and ash trays, and a large kitchen saucer in which were a few drops of liquid. And there were seven oranges, cut in halves, and apparently squeezed out. They were on a plate.

'The table was set in the middle of the room. *In the centre of it on a piece of black velvet ten inches square, fifteen large pigeon-blood rubies threw deep crimson gleams at the chandelier directly above them.*

'*And, in a circle round the table there sat in four chairs, four dead men, with their eyes closed, in the stifling hot and oppressive room, with the light beating down, and the rubies winking up at them.*'

Sir Edward's voice died away. The spell-bound silence which held the Dilettantes was broken by a gasp from Sir Noël Maurice.

'God bless my soul!' he said. 'Four of them? Dead!'

'Every man jack. Two were lolling back in their chairs held in place by the arms. A third was bent forward with his head resting on one arm, and the fourth had slipped half under the table.'

'What a scene for a stage curtain-opener,' Purcell said. 'Better than a Christie thriller!'

'How long he and Lombarde stood in the doorway hypnotized by the Grand Guignol setting Kenway said he didn't know. They were jolted into action by a shriek from behind them, and the servant — his name was Enrico Tiberti — fell in a faint.

'The first job was to ascertain the cause of death. A police doctor soon settled that; the men had drunk enough morphine to kill twenty people.

'By the time this had been ascertained the servant had recovered and was able to describe the morning's events.

The three men had been expected, he said, and arrived at 11.30. (We found later that they had left the train at Menton and motored from there to avoid the long train wait at the frontier station of Ventemiglia). When they reached the Villa two other people were there, a Signor Rossetti and his fiancée, Signorina Capponi, friends of his master. The company were introduced to each other and all had drinks at the same time, the drinks coming out of the same bottle. The Italians left at 12 midday and his master and the three men then closed the door of the room. That, Tiberti said, was the usual procedure on the visits of the three Englishmen. They used always that room and he (Tiberti) was under strict orders never to enter it or allow anyone else to do so on any account until he was called to speed the departing guests. The orders had been faithfully carried out that day as on other days: *nobody had gone in, and nobody had come out.'*

'What about the staff?' James asked.

'The only staff apart from Tiberti was a part-time cook who never arrived before 4.30, cleaning women from outside who came at 7 o'clock and were away by 10, and a secretary, by name John Garner, who had lived in Italy for three years, and had been Martini's secretary for that time. He was not in the house at the time, but materialized at 3.50, and seemed to go into a daze when told of the deaths. He explained that always on those days when the three men came visiting his employer, he was sent away and told not to return until 4 o'clock (This was confirmed by Tiberti). He had spent the morning since 10.30 and the early afternoon with a girl at Diana Marina, a holiday resort a few miles away.'

'So — the only person in the entire house apart from Signor Martini and his three guests was Tiberti,' James said.

'That's so — by design of Martini himself. Now, we are coming to the investigation, and you'll see what I mean when I say we were — and still are — entirely baffled by the deaths.'

13

'JUST a moment, Sir Edward.'

The interruption came from Purcell. 'You said there were four glasses on the table. But six people had had drinks. What happened to the other two glasses?'

'They were on the sideboard, but I'll be coming to that,' the A.C. replied.

'A little later,' the chairman said. 'I feel, after visualizing that room that I could do with something to pull me together. Would anyone join me in coffee?'

There being general acceptance, Emile, the waiter, was summoned and supplied their wants. To his wavering request 'black or white' all six Dilettantes chose black. Not until the cups had been drained, and cigars pushed round again, did the chairman wave permission for the strange tale to be continued. Sir Edward took up from where he had been halted.

'Lombarde and Kenway, understandingly, began with the glasses and the bottle. Who had handled them? They were dusted over and photographed, and the prints developed. Rollings of the dead men's fingers were taken and impressions of Tiberti's and the cook's. The results were this — the glasses from the table had Tiberti's finger-prints, as was to be expected since he had carried the glasses into the room and distributed the drinks. The two glasses used by Rossetti and his woman friend also bore Tiberti's prints and those of the Italian couple. Each of the four glasses had, also, the prints of the men in front of whom they had stood. *And they had no other prints.* The glass water-jug had the prints of Tiberti in several places and a conglomeration of prints, superimposed on the handle. Only two were distinguishable — one of Martini himself and one of Lord. The bottle of Cinzano had prints of all the men, as well as of Tiberti.'

'So the inference is that the bottle of Cinzano was passed round, and then the jug of water,' the pathologist ventured.

'That is so. The saucer, a large kitchen one, had been handled only by Martini. The rubies showed no sign of handling at all. Now, we come to the inside of the glasses. They had been emptied, but there were sufficient dregs in each to reveal the presence of morphine — and the amount found, worked out in ratio to a full glass of liquid, gave us the approximate dose of morphine each man had swallowed. Subsequent post-mortem analysis confirmed the amount — roughly twelve grains in each body, and three grains is a fatal dose.

'There was no morphine in the bottle of Cinzano, and there was none, either, in the jug of water. Nor in the oranges. But there was morphine in the liquid in the saucer. The most thorough search of the men's clothing and other possessions, of the room, and indeed of the house failed to disclose any container of any kind that had held morphine. The only other thing extraneous to the room was a screwed-up paper bag in a waste-paper receptacle. It bore the printed name and address of a Victoria Street, London, fruiterer, and had obviously held the oranges.'

'There was no other way into the room?' asked Charles. 'A secret panel, perhaps?'

'I'm afraid not.' The A.C. smiled. 'It's too old a trick to elude my birds! There was, however, another door from the room. It opened into a short passage off which was a marble-walled and floored wine cellar. This was well stocked with bottles, and a small refrigerator for cooling the champagne, etc. A door at the far end gave entrance to the kitchen. As you may guess this was pretty thoroughly investigated. The kitchen door was locked on the passage side, and the key was in the lock. There was no sign of its having been tampered with — Kenway thought of pliers being used to turn the key from the outside: you can't do it without leaving traces. In any case the kitchen door leading to the yard was also locked on the inside and the only person other than Tiberti who held a key to it was the cook.

'Finally,' the A.C. went on, 'we come to the *dramatis personae*. Signor Martini was well established in San Remo and known to be a man of considerable means, with a liking for a gay life. He was financially interested in building, selling and letting apartments — flats to us — which was the main activity of the secretary, Garner. Enrico Tiberti, who was always a suspect, was known to the police as an honest, if somewhat simple little man, of excellent character; and anyway Lombarde felt, and I agree with him, that he could be dismissed from the case if only for the fact that nobody sane would kill his master and three guests with only himself in the house. The cook, who had the only other key giving entrance to the Villa through the kitchen, had been in the bosom of her numerous progeny all day; and each of the two charwomen had equally cast-iron alibis.

'There remains the two who were in the Villa when our three men arrived, and the secretary. Signor Rossetti said he had been a close friend of Martini for some years. He had just become engaged to Signorina Capponi, and as they were in the vicinity of the Villa he called on Martini to introduce his fiancée. He gave us a clear and lucid description of the company in the room, and of the events leading up to his departure. Our three men arrived, he said, and were greeted warmly, as old friends, by his host. Drinks were suggested, and Tiberti was called in to mix them. He emptied a half-empty bottle of Cinzano, carried six glasses to the sideboard, poured the aperitif into four of them, opened another bottle for the other two, and gave each guest and his master a glass. He then went round with the jug and topped up each glass according to the wishes of the drinker.

'Signorina Capponi agreed with the description. Rossetti said it was obvious that the three men had come to talk business with Martini, so as soon after the drinks as etiquette permitted, he and his girl friend left. There were no oranges or rubies on the table then.

'As for Garner, the secretary, his story that he had been with a girl in Diana Marina was supported by a dozen people, and the time of his arrival back at the bus stop nearest to the Villa — in the Corso Garibaldi — was corroborated by the conductor of the coach, who knew him well. Garner said he knew nothing of the Englishmen's business with his employer, and did not even know the men. He had never been in the Villa when they arrived, but he always knew when they were coming, because of his employer's orders to clear out and not return before 4 o'clock. He knew of no enemy who was likely to wish Martini out of the way.

'That's all!' Sir Edward relaxed in his chair. 'That is our perfect murder — with five questions to which all our modern detective skill, and that of the Italian police, have failed to find the answers:

1. *How came four men, alone in a room, to be poisoned with morphine?*

2. *How did morphine get into their glasses when there was none in the Cinzano or in the jug of water? Remember that the glasses had already once been filled and drunk from, without harm.*

3. *How did the murderer get in or out of the room, remembering there was no entrance from the rear, and Tiberti, the whole time, was sitting a couple of yards away on his porter's chair by the hall door?*

4. *Who was the murderer, remembering that there was nobody in the house, so far as we could discover, except Tiberti?*

5. *Finally — and this is the greatest riddle of all — Why were they murdered? If it was for what the three men were bringing — and for what else should it be, to be planned for that day — why did the murderer leave the £6,000 worth of rubies behind?'*

14

THE atmosphere developed in the Dilettantes' Club when Sir Edward picked out a cigar and proceeded to light it as indication that he had reached the end of his capitulation of the events in San Remo resembled in miniature that in the auditorium of a theatre when the curtain descends on the first act of an Alfred Hitchcock thriller. James and Purcell tapped an appreciation with the bottoms of their glasses on the table, and this was followed by a buzz of comment. The chairman voiced the general feeling.

'It is an intoxicating problem, Edward,' he said, 'certainly the most interesting, even enthralling, you have ever given us.'

'The most incomprehensible, I should say,' Purcell put in. Charles said: 'Did I believe in the supernatural, this would strengthen that belief— only, I don't!'

The chairman brought the members to heel. 'Passing phrases is not of much benefit, gentlemen,' he rebuked. 'We meet here to debate problems and come to an opinion about them. Since the best criminological minds of two countries have failed to find a solution to this one, we are hardly likely to do so; but I think a theory or two might bring interesting intellectual gymnastics.' He addressed the A.C. 'In effect, Edward, it seems to be a variation of the Locked Room, does it not?'

'Very much so,' the A.C. agreed, and glanced at the professor who was concentrating on brushing specks from his lapels and did not see the challenge. James, whose branch of Science was also criminal and akin to that of the A.C., coughed.

'Two points occur to me, Sir Edward, but I expect your men have covered them — concerning the left rubies. Stones of that size and value — £6,000 I think you said — would be very hard to get rid of, a thing which undoubtedly the murderer knew. Were there any other valuables concerned with the three men which were taken? Secondly, had a deal been done, and the money paid over. And was that money taken?'

'Points of importance, James,' the A.C. agreed. 'They were, in fact, considered. There were three things against them. Firstly, each of the men had well-filled wallets in their pockets. Martini was carrying £300 in lira. Secondly, he had not drawn any considerable sum of money from his bank previous to the meeting with which to make any payment. Thirdly, Barker, the London character whose information had been correct in every detail, said distinctly that the three were carrying rubies stolen from

Thorill Hall. Had they had anything else I think he would have mentioned it.'

'Quite.'

Charles leaned back from the table and looked away from the A.C., as though a little diffident about what he was about to say. 'I had an idea half-way through Sir Edward's account,' he announced. 'But thinking it over now it sounds rather childish.'

'A little child shall lead them, Charles,' the A.C. said.

'What *was* the idea?'

'Obviously Martini was a crook, and more obviously the three men were crooks. But Martini had a pose as an upright citizen. Suppose, playing on that, they were blackmailing him. He tried to get rid of them and something went wrong?'

'I-in h-his own h-house! Three b-bodies!' The professor spoke for the first time.

'I was thinking of the trick of poisoning someone's glass, and that someone, sensing it, changing the glasses round. But I realized there were too many glasses.'

Silence overtook the debate. The chairman essayed to revive it. 'We do not seem to have revealed much originality so far,' he chided. 'Surely we can do a little better. Can we not call up an unseen killer — one carrying the Hand of Glory, for instance, moving invisibly among people? No? Then we must rely on sound reasoning. Professor, here you have a murderer who kills four people in a room which he never entered nor left. If ever there was an illogical proposition this is it.'

Complete silence greeted the challenge — an uncomfortable silence.

'Professor!' the chairman called.

Stubbs opened his eyes. 'I h-heard you Mr. Chairman,' he admitted. 'I w-was t-thinking.' He sat back and producing his silver box, slowly took two pinches of snuff. Replacing the box in a waistcoat pocket, he placed the fingers of both hands fanwise together and gazed benevolently at the company through his thick lenses. With his shock of grey hair he looked more than ever like a goblin.

'An investigator of anything, physical or mental, should constantly be on guard against the effect of suggestion,' he began. 'Not only m-must all p-prejudice and p-preconceptions be avoided, b-but when information is received from outside, t-the actual undeniable f-facts must b-be c-carefully sifted from t-the inference w-which invariably accompany t-them.

'Here, w-we h-have three f-facts: f-four men are m-murdered since it is p-plain they d-did not c-commit suicide. The m-murderer was n-not seen. He left b-behind £6,000 in p-precious stones. Gentlemen, t-to investigate w-we m-must look first closely at t-the *mise en scène*. It is important t-that we f-find a use for everything t-that appears in such surroundings. If t-there is a b-bell on a t-table on the stage in a p-play we know it is t-there for someone to ring. If there is a d-desk with ink, a pen and paper, it is certain t-that someone is g-going to write something. The illustrations can be multiplied a hundred-fold.

'In t-this *mise en scène* t-the first thing t-that strikes me is t-that there are t-two pieces that are out of k-keeping — t-that have no obvious p-purpose. The g-glasses were t-there for d-drinking from; the Cinzano was t-there for supplying the drinks, and the water jug also. And t-the rubies, t-they were t-there to be bargained over.

'*B-but for w-what do you suppose w-were t-the saucer and the squeezed oranges?*'

'Orange in the drinks for flavouring,' Charles suggested.

'In Cinzano? Oh, no. And it is to be n-noted t-that the oranges were n-not eaten, gentlemen. W-when one eats an orange cut in half one sucks it and t-the flesh c-comes away from t-the skin. But these oranges had been squeezed. And t-they had been b-brought uneaten all the way from London to a country which grows oranges. When Sir Edward spoke of oranges I ask m-myself, why should three m-men buy oranges in London — *and never eat them*. It is a p-point to be considered.

'L-let us now look at these three m-men who because of s-suspicion of t-them are always so c-carefully searched at D-Dover and Calais by the Customs. T-they have nothing — no rubies. Yet in t-the Villa, t-there are the rubies!'

He sniggered and then shook with inward laughter, glancing at the A.C. with eyes twinkling behind his heavy spectacles. 'I h-have a c-confession, he stammered. 'I, Marcus Stubbs, h-holder of a C-chair in Logic, I h-have b-been a criminal. I t-throw myself on t-the m-mercy of Sir Edward. I have t-travelled very much in my life, and s-sometimes t-there are little t-trifles it is not desirable that the C-Customs should see. So when I leave the t-train I c-call a porter to c-carry my bag. At the Customs I s-say to him that it is n-not n-necessary he t-take the bag inside. I will have it. B-but here is my ticket for my sleeper and here is a bag of oranges which will refresh me on the long journey and I will not embarrass myself carrying oranges in the customs shed. You w-will be g-good enough to find for me my seat and put on it t-the oranges, and I w-will s-see you there. And so it is, and I g-give the so good p-porter five shillings, and very g-grateful he is. I put the oranges on the little t-table in my sleeper ready for my r-refreshment, and then in the Villa at San Remo I cut open the oranges and *from t-them I squeeze out the rubies*, which I had pushed in through a slit which may not be seen. I wipe them dry of juice and put them on t-the velvet for t-the appraisement of Signor Martini.'

15

THE rustle that whispers from people when taut nerves are suddenly relaxed stirred among the listening Dilettantes. A grimace twisted the mouth of Sir Edward Allen.

'I see,' he said. 'So simple and so innocent.'

The professor beamed. 'It is s-sim-plicity t-that is m-most successful, Sir Edward. W-what Customs man on a train seeing a passenger eating with enjoyment an untainted orange with a bag on which is the name of the fruiterer w-would suspect seven other oranges which promised further succulent enjoyment?

'So we h-have t-the rubies, and we h-have deleted one of the odd-men-out things — if it is p-permitted me to l-lapse into a slang. But I am w-wondering all the t-time of the other one — t-the saucer . . .' His voice sank away into silence and he stared through the forms of his companions, and on into space.

'T-there is an abnormality here,' he said when he returned to consciousness. 'No! No!' The negatives came sharply at the chairman about to speak. 'Not t-that the m-murderer went unseen into t-the r-room: it is seldom a m-murderer is seen; *but that t-the rubies should be on the t-table.* That is inexplicable. Why should a m-man so phlegmatically callous as to commit four murders: so steelily c-calm as to c-carry t-them through w-without leaving a t-trace — W-why should he t-then leave behind the fruits of his p-planning?

'Gentlemen, t-there is one explanation, and only one, that reason c-can p-produce for such a paradox: *because it w-was impossible for him to take them away.*'

'But — !' James leaned forward, and the professor turned to him, invitingly. 'Surely any such man before he plotted would ensure that he would be able to obtain the loot,' he said.

The professor nodded, but did not reply. Instead he continued: 'W-why c-could he not take them away?' The little goblin-like man beamed through his spectacles. 'That constitutes the second part of the argument. In logic there must always be a premise and then the argument, d-divided into its c-component parts. So I t-think again, carefully, without r-regard to inferences and suggestions, and it seems t-to m-me that here in this so lovely Villa t-there has b-been presented, handsomely, on a plate opportunity for murder. Consider: the h-house is empty except for a s-servant who m-must never g-go into that r-room without he is summoned; the secretary is sent away; the day women h-have d-departed, and the cook d-does not yet c-come.

'Four men argue in t-the r-room over a price. They p-pick up the bottle which is free of p-poison and pour Cinzano into their glasses from which they h-have once b-before drunk, and they pour water from t-the jug which also has no poison — and t-they die. And somewhere around them is one who p-provided the poison —'

'And who got clear, unseen, from a sealed room, Professor,' the chairman said. With a chuckle he added 'And there was nobody behind the opened door this time to come forward and join the two detectives, and there was no murderer in the room. You must account for that.'

The professor spread his hands: squat hands with thick, stubby fingers. 'Once again, Sir Noël, let us look for the simple answer, rather than the c-complicated p-problem of h-how a m-man administered p-poison and escaped f-from a r-room into which he had not entered and out of w-which he c-could n-not come unseen by the porter.

And the simple answer is t-that *t-the murderer did n-not escape because he was n-never in the room.'*

They stared at him. 'Never in the room?' the chairman said. 'Come, come Professor. Is he, then, a spirit?'

The professor smiled. His voice lost its soft, almost humble tone in the concluding words of the statement — it rasped out, hardly and challenging. Sniffing pinches of snuff he peeped above his spectacles at the faces of the Dilettantes, and seemed to be enjoying the reaction registered there. He waited for further protests, but the company were speechless in their surprise; and he turned to the A.C.

'Your inspector, Sir Edward, is a skilled and thorough investigator?' he asked; and the A.C. nodded his opinion.

'And he found nothing . . . n-nothing at all, of the presence, at any t-time in the r-room of another person?'

'Nothing — *except poison which killed four men, Professor:'* and the A.C. smiled.

'And a saucer, with, in it, a little water and morphine; and *which had no known purpose*, Sir Edward. Remember that! Always I p-ponder over this oddity — and the w-waiting rubies.'

'The *waiting rubies*?' the A.C. said.

'Indeed, the waiting rubies, Sir Edward. And then, presto! as I ponder the key clicks into the t-tumblers of my l-locked m-mind, and the d-door to t-the answer is open.'

'Yes?' the A.C. asked, softly.

'I see one w-who has n-noted the f-frequent visits of the three men, and the secrecy s-surrounding t-them — the emptying of the house of all save t-the manservant, guardian of the door. I see one w-who h-has learned the reason for visits — perhaps from spying on Signor Martini; or p-perhaps, and this is m-more p-probable, from English associates. And he schemes murder and a future with money to spare. Alas! t-that so b-brilliant a planning, such virtual c-certainty of success, should be overwhelmed by a stroke of crude ill-luck t-that surely comes upon a person b-but once in a lifetime — the ill-luck that sends a policeman all t-the way from England k-knocking on t-the Villa's door *at three o'clock* in the afternoon.' He sighed: '*Sequitur saperbos altor a tergo Deus,*' he said, and looked as though he was saddened.

'Consider, gentlemen, that room with four men who have been dead for two, three hours. They c-cannot be discovered because the servant must on no account go into the room unless he is called — and there is no voice left to call him. But at 4 o'clock the secretary will return from his ordered absence. What w-will he do? He w-will go to the room, open t-the d-door' — the professor was stammering very little now — 'and see his master and three men round the table, immobile. He will go to them, see they are dead, and will rush wildly out, raising the alarm, and calling for a doctor.

'*But, first, he will sweep up the rubies from the table and put them in his pocket — and who is to know that there had ever been any rubies?*'

'My God!' the A.C. said, shakily. The professor ignored him.

'And he will take, also, the saucer to the kitchen, unlocking the passage door, and then there is no saucer for an old, and fanciful Professor of Logic to worry over. Alas, a policeman comes to the house at three o'clock, and enters the forbidden room, and there are the rubies and the dead men and the saucer.

'But gentlemen, there is time yet for him to retrieve something. All is not lost. He cannot tell the police about the tragedy because he is not there at the time, but with a lady in Diana Marina, and the police go away with the bodies, perhaps, and lock and seal the room?' He looked at the A.C.

'Yes.'

'He goes to the kitchen and f-from t-there to t-the w-wine cellar' — the stammering had returned — 'and from the r-refrigerator he t-takes out a cube-tray, and t-this he w-washes with hot water, emptying it down t-the s-sink. *And t-there is n-no visible clue left of how four m-men c-came to d-drink morphine.*

'For, you s-see, g-gentlemen, he h-had noticed on m-many occasions what his m-master and guests drank in t-that h-hot close room, shuttered, and with b-blazing lights, w-where t-the Cinzano and the w-water became t-tepid. Always t-they cooled t-their drinks w-with ice, which Signor Martini fetched from t-the refrigerator a few yards in t-the passage, *c-carrying it in a saucer which lay ready to his hand.*

'Ice t-that h-had been water into which before he w-went away, t-the secretary had mixed t-the l-lethal d-doses of morphine in just s-sufficient cubes for cooling four glasses, and had put it back into t-the re-refrigerator to freeze.'

16

'I SEE you have another jewel haul on your hands, Edward,' the chairman said when the Dilettantes had settled themselves comfortably in their seats. Invitation sounded in his voice and the company waited in pleasurable anticipation for the response. 'Let me see, the *Evening News* says £20,000, the *Star* records £25,000, and the *Daily Mail* has whooped it up to £30,000.'

The Assistant Commissioner of Scotland Yard permitted himself a smile: if there was detected a certain amount of chagrin behind it, it might, perhaps, be excused in the circumstances; it was the third robbery within a few weeks in which jewellery had vanished from the enjoyment of its lawful owners: and seemed likely to remain so. 'That is so, Noël,' he admitted. 'The . . . er . . . slight discrepancy in what should be easily ascertainable facts is due, I am told, to news-editors' desire to have a better story than their rivals, and to the fear that those rivals will whoop up the figure in order to go one better. In actual fact, the amount given to the Gentlemen of the Press by the Press Bureau at Scotland Yard was £18,500, which is a quite sufficient sum looked at from any angle.' He fingered his cigar and gazed reflectively at the glowing end. 'There are certain odd phenomena attached to the raid' — he paused and eyed the faces turned towards him with ironical quizzing — 'if you would care to hear them.'

'Lead on, Macduff,' said Purcell the mathematician: and was echoed with heartiness by the remaining Dilettantes. The jovial, if not altogether erudite form of the invitation was due to the mellowing influence of a particularly satisfying achievement of the Moroni's chef. Turtle soup had been followed by *sole suprème* and that by *Quenelles,* a savoury and *Crêpe Suzette.* Burgundy with the soup had been succeeded by Château Nenin '45. The chairman had eyed the latter with enthusiasm 'Rare! Rare!' he said and his voice had sunk reverently. 'Incontestably one of the three great years, which is why one so seldom sees it served. And now the end' — the A.C. passed his Green Chartreuse beneath his nose, and took a sip. He replaced the glass on the table, and began:

'The robbery was a pretty well planned affair. The victims were Ambrose & Company in Conduit Street, jewellers of some standing. Their premises are well-guarded with steel grills at the windows, treble locks on the doors back and front and an anti-burglar device sounding an alarm at whatever entrance is made by doors or windows. The thieves, alas, broke into the rear of the tailor's shop next door and bored through a wall into the jewellery establishment — the burglar alarms were accordingly obligingly silent. The raid took place on Saturday night, so was not discovered until Monday morning when the shop opened for business.

'It might have been a pretty expensive visitation, for the firm carries something like £250,000 stock, but the greater part of this was in the strong-room; the stolen, and lesser valuable gems, had been locked in an ordinary safe.'

'Why not in the strong-room with the others?' Purcell asked.

'Because they were the window display pieces, and the manager and his assistant who always arrived first and had keys to the safe could spend the time before the arrival of the managing director on re-dressing the windows. Only the managing director had the combination to the strong-room, and he did not attend at the shop until after 10 o'clock.

'No attempt had been made on the strong-room door and it was this that gave us a clue to the raiders. The Yard records told us that the *modus operandi* of a certain group of men was to enter from an adjoining building and make for a safe. And the operator on safes of this crew was a character known to us as 'Lady Dan'.'

'God bless my soul — a woman!' the chairman said. 'Extraordinary.'

'Not a woman, Noël. A man.'

'Then why on earth 'Lady Dan'?'

The A.C. laughed. 'For the simple reason of his absorbing interest in every pair of trim ankles which came into his line of vision. Since he habitually walked with his head bent forward and downwards — a trait which he had tried, unsuccessfully to eradicate, because it enabled anyone who saw him in the vicinity of a robbery to give us a red-hot description beyond any question — it was usually ankles which he saw first.'

'I think I should describe 'Lady Dan',' he said, 'in order that you may have some idea of his character. He was a tall, slim but athletic type, and a dandy. His suits were always impeccable; they cost him £60 apiece at a Saville Row tailor. The trousers were immaculately creased, and his association of matching colours in suit, shirt, and tie would have won the admiration of that arbiter of men's fashions, *The Tailor and Cutter*. 'Lady Dan' was exceedingly proud of his appearance and of his ability to attract women.'

The A.C. chuckled. 'You may not believe it,' he said, 'but crooks have their problem child equally with honest folk. And 'Lady Dan' was a problem to his confederates. They found themselves because of this obsession compelled to elect a rota of bodyguard to ensure that his mind was kept off ankles and on the more important, and frequently less dangerous, activities of larceny until any planned operation was completed. For 'Lady Dan' had few equals in burglarious entry and was bread and butter and jam to his group, besides being one of the best disposers of stolen jewellery in the country.'

'By no means an unusual obsession,' James said with a grin. 'Even crooks can make fools of themselves over women.'

'Crooks more so,' the A.C. retorted.

'Had women ever landed him in trouble?' the chairman wanted to know. He ruffled his hair with his fingers, which with him was a sign of satirical interest.

'Several times, Noël. On one occasion after a job, and with his pockets full of loot, he dallied with a damsel, and subsequently had to walk home, being unable to find a taxicab at 2 o'clock in the morning. A constable picked him up on a charge of failing to give a good account of himself, and the loot was discovered when he was searched at the police-station. He went to gaol for three years. So you see how essential it was from his confederates' point of view that he should be saved from his folly! But we'd better get back to the robbery. I have deviated in order to give you a character sketch of 'Lady Dan' because of certain circumstances which will come into the story later.'

The A.C. sipped again from his Chartreuse and bored his monocle into a perfectly good left eye — an affectation which had for years made him a butt for witticism among his friends. He settled himself more comfortably in his chair, and continued his story, to which the Dilettantes had been listening with an absorption born of expectancy of drama to come. 'I told you that Records pointed unhesitatingly to 'Lady Dan' and his crew as the raiders (he went on), and we sent out for them. But Dan had vanished: 'narks' maintained that they hadn't seen him about the place for a month or more, and suggested we should look up one of his 'floozies' with whom he was probably having a good time. We descended suddenly on two of his messmates, a man named Bill Yates and another called 'Flash' Peters. They were easily available at their homes and both denied any knowledge of the raid. When the *modus operandi* was pointed out they retorted that if, indeed, 'Lady Dan' had done the job he had done it solo: which was absurd, since no single operator could have got through the wall in the time. But though we turned the couple inside out, and their premises upside down, we found no trace of any jewellery.'

'W-were t-there no f-finger-prints?' The professor asked.

'None. More than that, we probed their entire wardrobes — suits, shirts, vests, overcoats, shoes and socks. We took samples of dust from these and put the samples through the laboratory. All we wanted were a few particles of old dust and mortar which would correspond with the mess left in the jewellery establishment and the tailor's shop next door. There weren't any. So there we were. We had no evidence against the pair; and 'Dan' was missing, and probably somewhere with a pair of ankles.'

17

'Now, we come to the . . .' the A.C. paused, and rather elaborately examined the tip of his cigar. His eyes, peeping up at his fellows, noted the attitudes of expectancy combined with a slight exasperation at the delay in the movement occasioned by his hesitation. The professor was leaning forward over the table; James and Purcell sat stiffly upright. Charles, the psychiatrist was boring into him with his eyes; and the chairman had laid down his cigar, which in itself was sufficient demonstration of his absorption. The A.C.'s eyes twinkled mischievously; it was several seconds before he continued.

'We come to the first of the odd phenomena,' he said at last. 'The robbery, as I have mentioned, occurred on Saturday night. On Tuesday morning Scotland Yard received a telephone call from a Chief Detective-Inspector of the C.I.D. in Nice, on the French Riviera. They had on their hands, he said, an English visitor who had been found dead in a first-class sleeping compartment of the Blue Train when it arrived at Nice the previous midday. The passport which he had by regulation handed to the conductor of the coach when he boarded the train at Calais, described him as Frank Somerley, born in London. But when his body and a suitcase was searched for an address, three other passports were found. The names in these were Delancourt, Faber and Timothy. The photograph in each was of the same person. That did not surprise us; nobody knows better than Scotland Yard how simple a matter it is to obtain a passport in any number of names, if you know the way to go about it, which makes passports pretty well an international farce. What Nice wanted to know was — which of the passports was genuine; and would we trace the relatives of the deceased, and give them the sad news.

'Well, we checked on Records in case he was someone known to us in either of the aliases, but found nothing. Accordingly we asked Nice to send us the coded fingerprints of the corpse. Imagine our surprise on receiving the prints to find that they belonged neither to Somerley, Delancourt, Faber or Timothy, but to a Mr. Delano Mortimer, otherwise, 'Lady Dan'.'

The A.C. leaned forward in his chair and let his monocle drop to the full check of its ribbon. He selected a cigar from the silver box on the table, inspected it carefully and proceeded to light it. Not until he was satisfied with the evenness of its burning did he resume his easy lounging in his chair, and continue his story. And then he appeared to diverge from the theme of 'Lady Dan'. 'Do you know what is a 'drummer'?' he asked. 'No? Well, he is an individual in the underworld who spots out likely places to rob, and sells his information as a marketable commodity. Such a man is Jake Ackerson, well-known to us.

'At the precise moment, or thereabouts, that we were talking to Nice, 'Drummer Jake' was talking to a C.I.D. man in the West London Hospital. He had staggered into the hospital with head and face wounds, as well as a broken rib or two, and was taken off to bed. There he bellowed for a 'dick', and when the doctors understood what he meant, they telephoned the police. A detective-sergeant and a constable waited on him and to them he told the tale of his injuries. He said he wanted to 'nark' on the Ambrose job and promptly told them 'Lady Dan' and his mob had cracked the joint and 'Lady Dan' was off abroad with the proceeds. He (Jake) had nosed out the crib, learned the security details, and sold it to 'Lady Dan' through his lieutenant, 'Flash' Peters, for £100 — to be paid on the completion of the coup. The money hadn't been paid over and he went round to 'Flash' Peters to collect it. That individual said he didn't know what he was talking about; the job had been planned by 'Lady Dan'. Jake thereupon told him what he thought of him, adding emphasis to the opinion by kicking him in the stomach, whereupon Peters had beaten him up. He was now, he said, going to send 'Flash' Peters down for a 'handful', not only as a means of getting his own back, but as a warning to any gentlemen in the future who might feel inclined not to comply with their bargains — to use a Stock Exchange cliché.'

'Handful, meaning prison, of course,' the chairman said.

'More than just prison, Noël. In crook slang a 'handful' means a five-year sentence. Jake knew that 'Flash' had a number of convictions and that the next one would bring him automatically, a five year stretch on the Moor. But to continue: within a few minutes of leaving the hospital the sergeant was through to the Yard with the story. It placed a very different complexion on 'Lady Dan's' death; the corpse of an Englishman in a French train was purely a matter for the French police. But 'Lady Dan' and £18,000 worth of stolen jewellery was very much our pigeon. We sent Detective-Inspector Kenway and a sergeant over to Nice in a chartered 'plane.'

18

'AND got the jewellery back,' Charles said with a chuckle. 'What a turn-up for the book! A chance death and —'

'We did not,' the A.C. corrected. He gazed ruefully at the ceiling. 'The French people were flabbergasted when Kenway asked what they had done with it. They had not seen any jewellery. Told the details, they started a grilling of all the people they had previously merely questioned about the dead man's movements the previous night. But — have a heart, you fellows. Talking is dry work. Do you think, Noël, we might have some of Moroni's excellent coffee?'

For a few moments talk became general, and trivial, and the A.C. relaxed. Not until cups had been emptied did the chairman remind Sir Edward of the stage at which he had arrived before the break. The A.C. replaced his monocle, and carried on with the tale.

'The bare facts of the discovery of 'Lady Dan' are simple,' he said. 'He went into his sleeper at 11.30 p.m. After the train reached Marseilles in the morning the coach conductor knocked on the door and called out the station and the time. He repeated the warning subsequently on several occasions, and when at Nice, where 'Lady Dan' had booked, there was no sign of activity he banged on the door, shouting *'Ici, Nice, M'sieur'*. Still getting no reply he became alarmed and called a gendarme. The door was forced open, and there was Dan, dead.

'Fortunately, the coach was one disconnected at Nice — is was a through coach booked there only. The remainder of the train went on to Monte Carlo, Menton, and over the border to Ventimiglia, with a single coach continuing on an Italian train to San Remo. So it was available for Kenway to inspect, having been shunted to a siding. I can give you a descriptive picture of 'Lady Dan's' compartment. You probably are familiar with the interior of a first-class sleeper on the Blue Train — the single bed, enclosed washbowl, racks for luggage, and the racks alongside the door for holding drinking-water jug and tumblers. On the side facing the bed is a door communicating with the adjoining compartment which if two are travelling together is open, but otherwise is bolted on each side. There was only one point that Kenway noted as of particular interest to him: on the little table beneath the window was a half full bottle of champagne and two tumblers. Each contained a few drops of champagne —'

'Ah!' James, the pathologist interjected. 'I see. He invited someone into the compartment — a confederate probably. The man killed him and decamped with the jewellery.'

The A.C. grimaced. 'So Kenway presumed at first, James,' he said. 'The French police surgeon quickly undeceived him.'

'How?'

"Lady Dan', you see, was not murdered. He died from a heart attack.'

'What!' James said. 'I thought you were telling us a murder story with £18,500 as the motive.'

'I didn't say so. But it might well be a murder charge, still, if we are fortunate. The doctor said there were traces of a strong sleeping draught in one of the glasses. 'Lady Dan' had apparently taken it. A lot of people do who find it difficult to sleep in a train. The amount, the doctor said, was not of itself fatal but Dan had what he described as *mal du coeur*, and the drug had stopped his heart.'

'But the jewellery, Sir Edward?' Charles protested.

'Yes, the jewels. Quite so. You will probably be able to guess the first question Kenway asked when he saw the inside of the compartment.'

'Who had been his visitor?' Charles suggested.

'Yes — and the reply was a facer. The conductor said: 'No visitors, Monsieur.' Questioned, he said that he saw 'Lady Dan' go into the compartment just after 11.30, and heard him bolt his door. He (the conductor) did not leave his seat in the corridor of his coach all night — you all know where the conductor sits — and nobody either went in or came out of 'Lady Dan's' domain.'

'But the glasses — had they not finger-prints?'

'Yes. Both bore 'Lady Dan's' prints, but no others.'

'Why should he then want two glasses?'

'The drug traces were in only one glass. The French police's view was that he used one glass in which to mix his sleeping draught, and the other for champagne which he drank before or after the draught. Possibly, the one contained some champagne undrunk, at the time he wanted to take the draught. But let me continue: Kenway did not think too highly of the suggested explanation, and decided to probe deeper into the movements of Dan. And there, he learned some very odd facts — from the barman of the *salon* bar. You will be familiar with the bar — the settee seats under the windows along each side with tables in front. The leather arm-chairs in the corners, also with tables, and the stool seats in front of the bar itself. 'Lady Dan,' it seems, wandered into the bar after the second dinner which finished at 9.30. There were half-a-dozen men present — and one woman —'

'So!' the chairman said. 'A woman — and 'Lady Dan.' The old failing.'

The A.C. grinned. 'Listen to the description of the scene by the barman.' He produced a thin sheaf of papers from an inside pocket and read:

> *"The lady is alone in a corner, Monsieur. She not order any coffee or drinks. When the monsieur came in he look at her and sit down opposite, across the coach. She look at the Monsieur from under her eye-lashes. You know how it is, with a lady who does not wish to be lonely? The Monsieur, he look at me and wink the eye, and he crossed and sat beside her and then he calls for the drinks. At 11.30 the lady and he left the bar together.'*

'Kenway pressed him for any other details he may have noticed about the woman — and received a very strange reply. 'She was a very odd lady, Monsieur,' he announced.

> *"How was she odd?' Kenway asked: and the man replied: 'She look at nobody all the time she is in the bar. And all the time from Paris she wear the gloves. She wear them in the restaurant when she have eat, and she wear them in the bar. Yet it is very hot in the train. For Mesdames to eat with the gloves is that not odd?'*

'The car waiters confirmed the gloves, and the conductor said she wore them in her compartment. Mention of her on this occasion seemed to revive his memory in 'Lady Dan's' retirement to bed, for he said she was wearing her gloves when she and Dan came from the bar together and entered the sleeper coach. Asked to elaborate on this, he said they walked together half-way along the corridor, then: 'He say *bonne nuit* to Madame, and went into his compartment, and Madame, she go to *her lit*.' Kenway asked which had been her compartment. It was the one adjoining that of 'Lady Dan' on the further side.'

'It's taking shape, Edward,' the chairman sniggered, delightedly. 'Sex is rearing its ugly head. They each enter their own quarters. He has arranged to raise the catch of the closed door on his side, and she that on her's and hey presto, they can engage in *une nuit d'amour* without the conductor being aware of it.'

'The drop catch on Dan's side was down, Noël; and he could not have put it down after his heart attack; and why on earth should he put it down before?'

'You traced the lady, of course?' Purcell said.

'We tried to, Purcell. The name the conductor had taken from her passport was Liza Underwood. She had left the train at Cannes, to where she had been booked. The French police undertook to produce her within a couple of hours. The law in France requires hotels and all boarding establishments to collect the passports of foreign visitors on arrival and send them to the nearest police authority who after noting details, return them. Thus, it is an easy matter for the *gendarmerie* to contact any foreigner. But though Cannes was searched from hotel to *pension*, from apartment to boarding houses, no trace of Miss Liza Underwood could be found. Nor along the whole of the Riviera on either side of Cannes and as far as the Italian border was there anybody with a passport in that name. From the moment she collected her passport from the conductor and left the train at Cannes Liza Underwood disappeared as though she had never been.'

'And you have no trace of the jewellery,' the chairman said, musingly. 'It is, as you said, a case riddled with curious phenomena.'

'Tell me —' Purcell began: the A.C. halted him with a wave of a hand. 'There is one other point, before you start the argument,' he said. 'Inspector Kenway of course went to identify the body. He knew 'Lady Dan' quite well —'

'And, found it wasn't 'Lady Dan' at all,' Charles burst out, triumphantly. The A.C. looked accusingly at him.

'It was 'Lady Dan' all right. You've forgotten the tele-graphed finger-prints, Charles! It was the man's face that shook Kenway. Dan had died, as I told you, of a heart attack. But there was no sign of strain or agony on his face. He must have been cut off in an instant, in a flash. And his last expression had remained as in a photograph. It was, Kenway said, an expression which could only be described as of complete and utter *stupefaction*. The eyes were staring as though at something incredible, and the jaw was dropped. I quote Kenway's remark to me: 'A.C., he looked as Moses must have looked when he saw the Red Sea suddenly bank up on either side leaving a dry passage across it. When I saw him I realized for the first time what the word stupefaction really means'.'

The A.C. relaxed in his chair. 'That, gentlemen, is the story so far as we have been able to progress,' he said.

Charles thought for a moment. Then: 'You said a little while ago that the case might be one of murder, yet the man died from heart failure, Sir Edward.'

'Yes. The law says that if two people are concerned in the committing of a crime and one of them dies as a result of the association while thus concerned then that brings a charge of murder. The heart attack could have been induced by the committal of the criminal offence.'

The pathologist interrupted: 'The criminal offence in this case being, I suppose, the receiving of property known to have been stolen?'

'Yes,' Sir Edward said.

'You think she stole the jewellery from 'Lady Dan'?'

The A.C. waved his hands in exasperation. 'I don't know,' he said. 'All we do know is that the jewellery vanished, and she was the only person we have traced who had any communication with him from the moment he stepped on the train at Victoria. But if she did, how did she get into his compartment — *and leave it again.* The communicating door between the two was fastened *on 'Lady Dan's side* and on her side.'

'Suppose the man — knowing as we do his obsession for women — let her into his compartment, with her willing, and she took the jewels after he had died from his heart attack. She would be safe in going through his luggage.' Charles put the suggestion, thoughtfully.

'That is what we have presumed, Charles,' the A.C. said. 'But how did she fasten his door on the inside, and still get out, without the conductor seeing her?'

'Edward,' the chairman broke in. 'One point occurs to me.' The A.C. looked inquiringly. 'I suppose he really did have the loot? If he didn't, then the problem is answered.'

'Oh, yes. He had it. When we pulled in 'Flash' Peters, and confronted him with Akerman's 'squeal' he admitted everything — including the fact that 'Lady Dan' had gone over to France with the proceeds.'

'How?'

'Ah, well, he wouldn't tell us how Dan was getting it past the Customs people.'

'You still have no trace of Liza Underwood?'

A wry smile chased a way across the A.C.'s face. 'We have even less trace than before, Noël,' he said. *There has never been a passport issued to a Liza Underwood.*'

'Bless me! Do you mean the passport was a forgery?'

'That is so. There's quite a profitable black market in forged passports, particularly British.'

19

'EDWARD, I don't see how you are going to get much further.' The chairman introduced a note of polite concern in the statement. 'The jewellery is somewhere abroad, Dan is dead, and you can't find the woman who may know the answer, and may have the jewellery.'

'Well, that's all I can tell you, Noël. You know as much as we do ourselves. It is possible, of course, that 'Lady Dan' cached the loot somewhere to collect later when he had thrown us off the scent with his trip abroad. Or he may have passed it to a confederate on the French side of the Channel. It's a matter for conjecture; and so is the woman. I've given you all the facts. If your combined analytical brains can discover anything we haven't — I'll be glad to hear it.'

A contemplative silence was broken after a few moments by Purcell. 'As I see it, Sir Edward, you have presented us with another of your dashed locked room problems — only this time it isn't a room, but a train compartment.'

The A.C. nodded. The chairman looked towards the bottom of the table — at Marcus Stubbs. 'Come, Professor,' he urged. 'You haven't said a dozen words as yet. What happened during that night in that sealed compartment? Can your logic get the fair Liza in and out of it, with a haul of pretty stones? Remembering always that the coach conductor was never more than a few yards away from the compartments?'

The professor had been slouching back in his arm-chair, his eyes hidden behind his thick lenses and his dropped head. Thus addressed, directly, he straightened up and peered at the chairman from under his shock of unruly and greying hair. Watching him, Sir Noël thought he looked more like a goblin than ever. Presently:

'Gentlemen' (he said) 'I shall always be grateful that you admitted me to this company. It is my greatest pleasure in life to join with you here and apply my mind with yours to the problems that are postulated. It is exercise of t-the m-mind only t-that g-gives incentive to life, and youthfulness to age. Age is not the emaciation of the body b-but t-the atrophy of the mind. Consider t-the dejection, t-the Slough of Despond in w-which must l-live one whose m-mind from non-usage is atrophied: who sees without seeing, heârs without hearing, and r-roams amidst erudition w-without understanding.' He raised his head, big and seemingly unwieldy on the little body. 'Gentlemen I d-drink to you all with m-my appreciation of the Dilettantes.' He emptied his glass.

The embarrassment which comes always to men hearing themselves eulogized was broken by the chairman. 'That, my dear Professor, is very nice of you, but quite unmerited,' he said. 'I assure you we are as delighted to have you as you apparently are to be present with us.' The professor bowed acknowledgment, and spoke again:

'Of all the intellectual labyrinths presented for our consideration none is more tortuous than t-those from Sir Edward. Fortunately, he leaves us, usually, the thread of Ariadne as a clue from the centre of the maze to the exit. T-the immediate p-problem is no less enigmatical t-than t-those of the p-past.' He felt in a waistcoat pocket, produced the silver snuff box and sniffed delicately from a pinch of the contents, flicking away grains from a coat lapel. And he took a sip from his chartreuse, afterwards setting down the glass with a little grunt of satisfaction. Then he resumed:

'B-but, gentlemen, t-there are certain aspects of the recital of Sir Edward w-which are not in a-accordance with logical convention; and rules w-which do n-not c-conform

with, or are alien to logical explanation are impossible
— and, therefore, unacceptable. L-let me illustrate: it is
not logically possible, or even conceivable that one may
disappear from a locked room without having entered it
— or enter it without leaving. Nor is it p-possible t-that a
m-man should die w-with tremendous surprise on h-his
face if he had not seen s-something thus to startle him.
And w-what w-was there then t-to startle a man in a sleeping c-compartment which he h-had been occupying since
he left Calais at 2 o'clock the p-previous afternóon?'

'I listened with attention to Sir Edward's recital, but
more greatly t-to the oddities in it. It is t-the odd things that
betray the impossible. It was t-the oddity of a thread lying
on the g-ground t-that guided Theseus through the Cretan
maze. And in the riddle which Sir Edward has provided
to-night the oddity is the lady. *Cherchez la femme*.' The
professor paused: he seemed to the watching men to be
collating his thoughts. Presently, he arrived at a formula,
and proceeded: 'C-consider the f-facts we p-possess. 'Lady
Dan' who in his obsession for women w-will forego his
w-work, his p-personal safety: even betray the interest
and w-welfare of his friends. Fleeing from justice w-with a
fortune in his p-possession he g-goes into a bar, and t-there
is a lady and, inevitably, he joins her. Why should he not?
Why should not any of the six men in the b-bar have joined
t-the lady who sat alone in a c-corner, with no drinks in
front of her? Recall, g-gentlemen what the b-bartender
said: 'She look at Monsieur f-from under her eyelashes.
You know how it is. Monsieur, with a lady who does not
w-want to be alone.' Indeed, I know how it is; I w-was not
a s-stranger to t-the inviting look in my student days.' He
grimaced: 'B-but not any longer,' he added.

'Is it not strange t-that the lady who does n-not w-want
to be lonely, w-who is prepared readily to r-respond to

a g-gentleman's amatory advances, g-gave no inviting g-glances to any of the six men already in the b-bar: *but k-kept her p-proffered favours until the predacious 'Lady Dan' arrives?'*

'A pick-up?' Charles said.

'Deliberately,' put in the chairman.

'Planned, you m-might suppose by someone possessing k-knowledge of t-the jewellery?' the A.C. broke in.

The professor ignored the questions, and continued with his thesis. 'There is an odd t-thing about this odd lady — she wore gloves always — in the r-restaurant, in t-the bar, in her c-compartment.'

'Perhaps she had eczema, or something,' Charles suggested, and was ignored.

'Once in Monte Carlo I knew a w-woman who wore gloves always —'

'Monte Carlo — you, Professor!' The surprise in the chairman's voice brought a smile to the face of the queer little man.

'In my young and wild days, Mr. Chairman. She was a very lovely girl whom an English peer had seen w-working in t-the fields in Italy, and h-had t-taken to be his mistress. Her skin golden-cream from the sun was flawless, her hair and her eyes wonderful; only her hands, ravaged by hard work in the fields from a child w-were b-beyond repair by t-the b-beauty parlours. So she was never seen without gloves. *W-what c-could it be, g-gentlemen, in t-the hands of the w-woman in the Blue Train t-that would betray her, were t-they ungloved?'*

The professor paused for his periodical and inevitable pinch, and the usual flick of traces of brown from his ancient dress-jacket. 'So w-we progress to the second of our k-known facts, he continued. "Lady Dan' and his g-gloved *inamorata* leave the b-bar and walk to the sleeping coach, and go into their respective compartments. Nine hours later 'Lady Dan' is d-discovered dead. The l-lady has left the train at Cannes, shortly before. In the c-compartment of d-death are half-a-bottle of champagne and t-two tumblers.'

He looked slowly round the five men, until his eyes rested on the face of the A.C. 'Gentlemen, it is in the n-nature of d-detectives t-that they w-will theorize on w-what *might* have happened — and not only detectives — instead of accepting the simple facts staring at them, however difficult they may appear to be — so the t-two t-tumblers are accounted for by saying that the m-man p-probably used one for mixing his sleeping draught and the other for drinking h-his champagne. Yet, how easy is it to accept the obvious, as did Inspector Kenway at first: he asked 'Who w-was his visitor?' And accepted the answer: 'Nobody went in or c-came out, the conductor was in t-the c-corridor all the t-time.'

The professor halted, and looked down at the table. He lifted the coffee pot, poured out a cup-full, and drank it slowly. He settled himself back in the chair. 'I put myself in t-the skin of 'Lady Dan'' (he proceeded) 'who is a ladykiller, w-with a lady p-prepared to be k-killed, so to speak. I s-say to the l-lady: 'You are n-next door to me. T-there is champagne in my c-compartment, and a little *divertissement*, perhaps. You lift the c-catch on your s-side of the d-door and I w-will lift mine — and we are one'. So t-there are t-two glasses, gentlemen. Simple, is it not?'

Sir Edward stayed him. 'You forget, Professor, that the catch was secure on 'Lady Dan's side — and nobody left his compartment. And in any case his corridor door was locked on the inside.'

'I do n-not forget it, Sir Edward. Neither d-do I forget the look of stupefaction on the face of the d-dead man, or the vanishing into thin air of t-the woman who w-was always gloved, and who s-schemed to be p-picked up by 'Lady Dan' — and by nobody else. See how the tumblers of reasoning fall into their g-grooves and s-set the m-machinery moving to unlock the d-door.

'The locked and sealed compartment? — phiff! it is simple when t-the facts are considered.' He made a moue. 'It is long since I travelled by the Blue Train, but I r-remember those c-communicating doors very well. The catches were of heavy metal and t-they d-dropped into deep slots on each s-side of the door. It is so, still?'

The A.C. nodded agreement.

'So, if one sets such a catch balanced a little, ever so little, out of the perpendicular, pulls the door so gently until it is about to be closed, and then at the last jerks it violently shut, *the catch obeying, as it must, the law of gravity will drop into the slot and, behold, you have a locked door.*'

He sat back. A beneficent smile beamed all over his face, and he waved his hands in the air like a child delighted at the successful issue of a trick. Sir Edward was staring at him, brows puckered, head nodding slightly as though he had arrived at a considered decision. 'It could be so,' he said. 'You think. Professor that that is the explanation, and that she has the jewellery?'

The professor looked at him over his spectacles. A smile played round his eyes. 'You do not, even yet, Sir Edward, carry all the facts t-to their logical c-conclusion. Like the words of the hymn, one step enough for you — never the distant scene.'

'Meaning by that?'

'You s-search for a woman you cannot f-find, and w-whom you w-will never find.' He ceased speaking and had resource, again, to his snuff box. He pushed back the mop of hair, fallen over his forehead, and refreshed himself again with coffee — now cold. Then:

'I will look into m-my c-crystal of logic and describe to y-you what h-happened in that c-compartment t-that night.' He cupped his hands round an imaginary article on the table in front of him and peered. 'Ah! it is v-very c-clear,' he said. 'I see the c-catches lifted and t-the door opened and Miss Liza s-steps in as all along she h-had p-planned. The man is in the t-throes of expectation. He pours out t-the champagne. I see Miss Liza empty a phial of liquid into his glass as his back is turned. And t-they d-drink and t-talk. I see, presently, t-the man begin to feel d-drowsy and suggest t-the time has come for the *divertissement*. I hear the w-woman laugh quietly and see her turn her back and take off the blonde hair, and t-the g-gloves hiding the hands which w-would have betrayed her. For, g-gentlemen, when she t-turned round again, *It w-was t-the face of a man that 'Lady Dan' saw*.'

'A man!' The chairman shot up in his seat.

'But, of c-course. How else c-can you account for the look of stupefaction on his face? Had a woman asked h-him for the jewels, he would have been, not stupefied, but very angry. But a man! Whom h-he h-had been courting! The shock to his ego and self-esteem, so sudden and unexpected a shock combined w-with t-the action of the d-drugs together on his heart killed him. Did not the doctor say the drug was not in itself lethal but that he had a bad heart?'

'A man!' the chairman said again.

The professor turned to the Assistant Commissioner: 'Forget t-the w-woman, Sir Edward,' he said. 'Look for a man.'

Extracts from the *'Daily Record'*.

Inspector Kenway said: 'When the prisoner was arrested and charged with taking the jewellery he replied: 'All right. It's a cop. But I wouldn't have thought 'Lady Dan' would squeak on his Liza! He'll be a laughing-stock, when the case comes on. He'll never live it down. Put it over him properly, did pretty Liza. The things he said to her! And his face was a picture when my golden curls came off.' The prisoner did not know that the man had died until I charged him with causing his death . . .

His real name is David Randall. He is known to us as a thief with a long criminal record, though he is only 26 years of age. Until the present case his robberies had been committed in country houses where he posed successfully as a housemaid. All his employers spoke highly of the qualities of their maid until 'she' vanished with their valuables. In criminal circles he is known by the nickname 'Gracie'.'

20

'IT IS in my m-mind, Sir Edward, t-that t-there h-has been a grave miscarriage of justice.'

The professor peered at the Assistant Commissioner of Police of Scotland Yard through his thick lenses. And shook his goblin-like shock of hair.

The Dilettantes had dined epicurean-like off asparagus soup, sole *bonne femme*, pheasant with game chips and cauliflower *au gratin*, an oyster savoury and ripe Stilton in place of a sweet; and were now sitting over cigars and a Port of the 1927 vintage, bottled after twenty years in the wood. The time had thus arrived for their customary battle of intellect on any topic that might be introduced, or crop up in the course of general conversation.

They gaped at the professor! It was unusual for him to initiate any discussion; his habit was to be the last to offer any contribution — after he had listened to the arguments: sitting with eyes closed and head sunk between his shoulders, so that the Dilettantes were never quite sure whether he were awake or asleep. Then, his analytical brain satisfied with conclusions at which he had arrived, he entered the fray, frequently demolishing by pure logical reasoning an edifice which his fellow Dilettantes had erected; or building-up where they had pulled down.

It was recollection of his invariable accuracy of reasoning and the uncanny success of his expositions over the past few months that were responsible for the silence which now greeted his declaration. It was as though a cold douche had fallen on the gathering. Sir Noël Maurice, the chairman, was the first to find his voice.

'Miscarriage of justice! In connection with what, Professor?'

'W-with, of c-course, the c-conviction of John Parker for the murder of t-the w-woman, Mary Bloss.'

An awkward constraint held the Dilettantes mute. The professor had never been one to express an *opinion*: his views, when he spoke them, were postulated as conclusive: ad *amussim*. The clarion call was recognisable behind the tone of his voice now.

'He did not kill,' he said. 'Pfui!'

The trial of John Parker had been concluded a week previously; a sordid story of a married man and a liaison with another woman, clandestinely carried on. At the end of the first day's evidence — the trial had lasted three days — there was little doubt in the minds of the people in court — or those outside who followed the case in the newspapers — what the outcome would be. Mr. Justice Lorraine in passing sentence expressed his agreement with the decision of the twelve good men and true. He had summed up against the prisoner.

Sir Edward Allen stressed the point when he replied to the professor's challenge of the verdict. 'The jury seemed to entertain no doubts, Professor,' he said. 'They were out only half an hour. The judge agreed. As far as the police are concerned I can assure you I had no doubt: had there been the slightest doubts in the minds of the investigating officers, Parker would never have been put on trial.'

The professor nodded his shock of hair. 'Of that I am sure, Sir Edward,' he admitted. 'It i-is n-not t-that I have c-criticism of your p-police.'

The intensity of his feelings had brought out his stutter. 'That there was a *prima facie* case I do not deny. The jury? They returned a verdict in accordance with t-the evidence g-given b-before them. Indeed, t-they could n-not have r-returned any other.'

'Then,' Sir Noël turned a furrowed brow on the little man. 'Then wherein lies the miscarriage of justice, Professor?'

'In the defence, Mr. Chairman.' His head nodded in emphatic protest: he thumped the table with a fist. 'Never, but never have I seen such futile incompetence, such a surrender of a man's freedom, if not his life — for it would mean his life had hanging not been abolished by your Parliament.' He turned to the A.C. 'You have a saying, Sir Edward, t-that one can drive a coach-and-four through your laws, have you not?'

The A.C. smiled. 'There is such a saying, yes. There are sometimes grounds for it,' he admitted.

'Sir Edward, one c-could d-drive a procession of c-coaches t-through the c-case against the man Parker. I will undertake t-to demolish it.'

'And find the murderer?' Sir Edward put the query.

'And point the *probable* murderer.'

The chairman rapped on the table. 'Gentlemen, if it pleases you, we have the opportunity for a unique session,' he announced. 'We will arraign John Parker before you. The professor shall conduct his defence.' He paused. 'That is, if you, Sir Edward feel qualified to put the case for the police?'

The A.C. nodded. 'I am in full possession of all the evidence,' he said. 'I judged it before the papers went to the Director of Public Prosecutions.'

'Very well. Then it is agreed?' There was a chorus of assent. 'Then I propose we refill the glasses and light a cigar, and then set ourselves in court.'

The box of cigars and the decanter were passed round. Then:

'Sir Edward,' the chairman invited.

The Assistant Commissioner drew on his cigar, and removed it from his lips holding it between thumb and finger. 'John Parker' (he began) 'was a partner with Herbert Morley in a business which supplied precision instruments to the engineering trade. It is a flourishing concern; with a factory and offices in Ealing, a suburb of London. Parker had a house in Gunnersbury Avenue, also in Ealing. He was married but without children. His partner lived at Harrow Weald, which is some five or six miles from Ealing. The partner plays only a small part in the drama which will be unfolded to you.

'The dead woman, Mary Bloss, was an old friend of Mrs. Eileen Parker, wife of the prisoner. She had, in fact, been a bridesmaid at her wedding; and used frequently to visit the Parker home.

'Parker had one hobby: he was an enthusiastic lepidopterist. In pursuit of this hobby he made frequent weekend trips to the haunts of moths, particularly the Norfolk Broads, taking with him nets, arc-lighting apparatus used to attract the moths to the nets, and killing bottles. These bottles were loaded with cyanide. And Parker had a stock of cyanide in his study at home, where he kept his considerable collection of moths mounted in glass cases. The fact, gentlemen, is important.'

Sir Edward hesitated. He appeared to be in some doubt how to continue. He took a sip of port. 'It is a matter of some difficulty to present a picture of the position to you,' he apologized. 'I will, I think, have to skip backwards and forwards over the evidence: that is, not present it in the order that the prosecution presented it in court. Perhaps I should start by explaining the domestic position of the Parker household as it was gained from certain witnesses, and our inquiries. The moth-hunting expeditions which I have mentioned play an important part.

'Mrs. Parker had become suspicious of her husband; those suspicions were aroused in a curious way. She had, at first, accompanied him on the trips, until she became bored with sitting half the night in reeds, whereupon she stayed at home. Parker used to return from the trips with dozens of moths, and spend the subsequent evenings in classifying his specimens, and setting them up in cases. But she had noticed that of late he was returning from his expeditions with nothing to show. She was convinced that the trips were being spent, not with moths, but with a woman. She, in fact discussed the point with the dead woman —'

'H-how do y-you k-know that?' the professor asked.

'From a Mrs. Marina Walters, who was a witness. She was a friend of Mrs. Parker and also of Mary Bloss. Mrs. Parker had confided her suspicions to the Bloss woman who, in turn, passed them on, in confidence (!) to Mrs. Walters. According to Miss Bloss, Mrs. Parker was determined to divorce her husband on the grounds of adultery —'

'With whom?' the chairman asked.

'With, she said, a woman unknown.'

'But she had no proof — or had she?'

'None whatever, which is what Miss Bloss said she told her. She had, however, found in one of her husband's suits, which she was about to send for cleaning, a bill for £10 for an article of jewellery which was certainly not in her trinket-case. Miss Bloss, according to Mrs. Walters, said all husbands go off the line occasionally, and it would be best to leave things alone: it would probably blow over. That is the background of the story.'

2 1

'Now, we come to the weekend of the tragedy.' The A.C. drew on his cigar and waited until the tip was glowing red. 'Mary Bloss (he continued) occupied a flat in a luxury block in Acton. She lived alone, doing her own cooking, but had a woman come in each morning to do the household chores. The woman, a Mrs. Loveday, had a key. On Tuesday morning she arrived as usual and called out good morning. Getting no reply she went into the bedroom, to find that the bed, though turned back in readiness for retiring, had not been slept in. She re-made it, and put the flat into order, and then went to the bathroom which it was her custom to leave to the last. There, she found

Miss Bloss on the floor, dead. A woman of some intelligence, she dialled 999, and left everything just as it was. A sergeant from Ealing station, who answered the call, took only a minute or two to decide on his course of action: he telephoned Scotland Yard and Detective-Inspector Kenway and a sergeant went along with a Murder Bag.'

Sir Edward poured out a glass of port and sipped from it. He fitted his monocle back into his perfectly good left eye, and after a glance round the faces of the Dilettantes centred on him in lively interest, continued:

'Mary Bloss lay on the floor of the bathroom. She was attired only in a nightgown. Judging by her position, Kenway concluded that she had collapsed partly on the bath, and then slumped on her back. A toothbrush was still held by the fingers of her right hand. On the floor, slightly under the wash-bowl was a tube half full of dental cream. I need not describe the medical symptoms . . . it is sufficient to say that death was due to poisoning by cyanide. She would have died instantaneously — within two or three seconds.

'The divisional surgeon put death as having occurred some eleven hours previously. As it was 9 a.m. when he examined the body, that would make the time of death about 10 o'clock the previous night. The point is significant: the woman had prepared for bed and was brushing her teeth before retiring when she collapsed. The brush and the tube were sent to the laboratory at Scotland Yard and both were found to contain enough cyanide to kill half a dozen people. The laboratory director said that the cyanide in liquid form, had been mixed with the dental cream, and when the latter had been squeezed on to the brush a lethal dose of cyanide had gone with it, and thus been introduced into the mouth. I should tell you that one taste of the poison is sufficient to cause almost instant death.

'We now come to the connection with Parker. Inquiry into Mary Bloss's movements revealed that she had told Mrs. Walters on Saturday she was going away for the weekend. The porter at the flats deposed that a car drove up to the entrance of the flats, and the driver tooted three times. That was at 9 o'clock. Miss Bloss's flat is on the first floor, over the entrance. The porter recognized the driver as a man who used to visit her, but he did not know him by name. A minute or two after the tooting Miss Bloss left the flats' entrance carrying a small case. She got into the car, which was driven off. On Monday, about midday the car drove up to the flats again. Miss Bloss stepped out and entered the flats. The car drove off. He did not, he said, see Miss Bloss again. She had no visitors, so far as he knew, and did not leave the flat. The girl on the flats' switchboard said that Miss Bloss had no in-coming telephone calls, but herself made a call shortly after midday. She could not recall the number, but it was a local call, otherwise she would have booked it.

'With the body removed Inspector Kenway began a search of the flat — that is, of course, routine. In the bedroom was a woman's night-case, fitted with bottles, etc. and partly unpacked. The flat porter subsequently identified it as the one Miss Bloss had carried to the car —'

'W-was it identifiable as b-belonging to the w-woman?' the professor interrupted. 'I mean did it contain identifiable information?'

'There were three letters addressed to her, which, judging by the postmarks, had arrived on the Saturday morning shortly before she left.'

The professor nodded. 'Ah!' he said. 'Please to continue, Sir Edward. I am s-sorry to h-have interrupted.'

'On the dressing-table was a paper bag containing a woman's scarf. With it was a receipted bill for 17/6. It bore the name of a drapery shop in Hickling, Norfolk. The purchase had been made on the Saturday —'

The chairman raised a staying hand. 'Edward has now been talking for a considerable time,' he said. 'It will be a charity to allow him a short respite. Meanwhile, we can inwardly digest the evidence he has placed before us so far. Is your fancy for a little of Morino's excellent coffee?'

He rang the service bell.

22

REFRESHED and rested Sir Edward resumed after five minutes. 'Let me see — where was I? Oh, yes. A scarf bought in Hickling. A telephone call to the shop brought the information that it was bought by a lady who was staying at the Fishers' haven, a small hotel in the village. The help of the Norfolk County C.I.D. was solicited and they came along with the information that the only two people who had stayed there during the weekend were a Mr. and Mrs. Parks, according to the registration. They had stayed there on several previous occasions. They arrived by car, the registration of which was OOX 0251. The number had fortunately been recorded by a young son of the house who collected car numbers. Scotland Yard quickly ascertained that the car was licensed to John Parker. Further information sent by the Norfolk police was to the effect that the couple had had high words on the Sunday evening. The words 'why the hell don't you get some moths, you bloody fool . . . Get out and don't let me see you again till the morning!''

'Whereupon, you, of course, questioned Parker?' Charles suggested.

'We did —'

'He admitted being at H-Hickling w-with the w-woman?' the professor asked.

'Yes. It would have been useless had he denied it. The porter at the flats identified him as the man who came with the car. In addition, the car itself, when we finger-printed it as routine, disclosed the prints of Miss Bloss, Parker himself, and of his wife —'

'Ah, his wife!' The professor looked up quickly. 'Ah! how did they get there?'

'I will come to that, presently, Professor. The car contained also a rug which Mrs. Parker did not identify as her property, but which Mrs. Loveday, the Bloss daily woman, said belonged to her mistress. The motive —'

The professor interrupted. 'No, no, Sir Edward,' he protested. 'You have not finished yet with Parker. You f-forget e-evidence w-which I read, and regard as most important. Oh, yes, most important.'

'What evidence, Professor?' The A.C. regarded the little man with amused benevolence.

'Of Parker's movements on his return from Hickling on t-the M-Monday.'

'He was with his partner the remainder of the day —'

'No, no, b-before t-that, Sir Edward, w-when he reached London.'

'He left Miss Bloss at the entrance to her flat.'

'And then?'

'He drove home, and —'

'This is what I am wanting. Little notice was p-paid to it in evidence. There was a little scene, w-was t-there not?'

'Yes. But it does not seem to have much bearing, Professor. Parker arrived home at 12.50 o'clock and found his partner walking up and down the drive in a rage, with Mrs. Parker trying to pacify him —'

'The t-trouble being?'

'A business deal to be negotiated in Bedford. Morley said it was a chance in a lifetime and he (Parker) was spending his time chasing blasted moths. To Parker's retort that he knew nothing of any possible deal. Morley replied that the offer had only arrived in the morning's post. They had now two-and-a-half hours to reach an appointment in Bedford to negotiate.'

'And t-they left together — in whose car?'

'In the partner's car. Mrs. Parker who was upset, said she would run Parker's car into the garage, and unload it of the moth-hunting kit. She urged him to hurry off. That, Professor' — the A.C. said, turning towards him — 'is how Mrs. Parker's prints came to be in the car, on the wheel, and along the back of the back seat.'

'She d-did empty t-the c-car — I remember.'

'Yes. From that time Parker was continuously in the company of his partner until the following morning; they spent the night in Bedford.'

He did n-not go into the f-flat w-with Miss Bloss?'

'No. He was already late, having had trouble with the car on the way, and he drove off as soon as the woman had left.'

'T-that, if I remember rightly from reading t-the evidence was h-his defence — t-that the woman was well when he l-left her; t-that she was known to be all right at 6 o'clock t-that night w-when she ordered a meal from the flats' restaurant?'

'That is so. It failed, of course. The alibi was useless, since the case for the prosecution was that following the quarrel in Hickling, Parker had syringed cyanide from his killing bottles into the tube of dental cream, knowing from her habits, that she would not be using her toothbrush until she was alone in her flat.

'To conclude — in the face of the evidence, and on the fact the woman had no callers and did not leave the flat after the return from Hickling; that only Parker possessed cyanide, and only he had been in her company, the police obviously had to arrest him on the murder charge.'

Sir Edward let the monocle fall from his eye. He sat back in his chair and pointed his cigar at the professor. 'The prosecution rests, my learned friend,' he said, with a smile.

The Dilettantes relaxed. They had been listening with marked mental concentration, now and then glancing at the professor, to see what effect the more damning pieces of evidence had on him. Now, they surrendered their attention and turned to their cigars, and another round of port in the interval. And to a gentle chaffing of the only one among them to sit silent.

The chairman allowed five minutes to elapse. Then he rapped on the table and announced: 'For an acquittal, Professor.'

The little man with the goblin-like shock of hair, started at his name; and looked up, sharply. A smile enlightened his face. He extracted the silver box from a waistcoat pocket, and sniffed delicately at a pinch from the snuff contents. With equal deliberation he flicked the traces of brown from his lapels, poured out a glass of port and slowly sipped it. His eyes did not leave the face of the Assistant Commissioner. The Dilettantes were watching him intently; he acknowledged it with a twinkle in the eyes behind the thick lenses of his steel-rimmed spectacles.

A minute — two minutes — passed, and he was still silent, the fingers of his right hand tapping the arm of his chair, his eyes still on the A.C. who fidgeted under the stare. Then he spoke, slowly and without a trace of stammer.

23

'WHY was the wife of Parker not called to the witness box, Sir Edward, do you suppose?' The query came softly.

'Why? . . . er . . . under our law, Professor, a wife cannot be called to give evidence against her husband,' the A.C. said.

'By the prosecution. Why was she not called by the defence?' The A.C. frowned.

'I can't answer for others,' he said. 'But I understood that defending counsel after reading through the depositions decided against calling her because of the possible danger to Parker if she were cross-examined by the Crown.'

'Idiots!' The professor snorted. 'She could have been the best possible witness for the man had the solicitors prepared a defence as they should have done. As I would have done,' he added, but under his breath, so that only Norman Charles, the psychiatrist, who was sitting next to him heard it. He went on, addressing the A.C.

'There are one or two small matters you understand that I am clearing the decks, so to speak. The rug that was found in the car: it was shown to Mrs. Parker?'

'Yes.'

'Why?'

'Why?' the A.C. repeated. 'Well, actually it was taken into the house by Inspector Kenway after he had examined the car to be identified as belonging to Parker, in the ordinary routine of inquiry concerning possession.'

'And Mrs. Parker identified it as belonging to Miss Bloss? She did not, for instance, say: 'It is not mine. Someone must have ridden with my husband and left it'.'

The A.C. frowned. 'I gathered so from Kenway. It was confirmatory evidence of occupation of the car by the woman. She said it belonged to Miss Bloss.'

'Quite. The inspector had, of course, examined the rug first and found no identification tag on it, hence his inquiry. Another matter, Sir Edward. Although you did not say so in your admirable review of the evidence, I am quite sure your excellent detective officers questioned the telephone switchboard operator about the call Miss Bloss made shortly after she had been decanted by Parker at her flat. I cannot believe that when they were searching for a murderer not then known that they would not quiz her in what the call was about. Is that not so?'

'As a matter of fact — yes,' the A.C. agreed. 'She said —'

The professor stopped him. 'A little later, Sir Edward. We will come to it in its proper context.' He looked round at his fellows: 'We have now cleared the air, so to speak, and we can investigate strange circumstances, starting with the murdered woman. Do you know her circumstances? For instance, the rent of her flat?'

'Twelve guineas a week — and rates.'

'And what did she do for a living?'

'Nothing.'

'You made inquiries concerning her and found she was of independent means — yes?'

'No. We found no known source of income.'

'But that she was a woman of the world, with a circle of friends almost all male?'

The A.C. nodded, frowningly. 'We were not concerned with her moral character, Professor,' he said. 'We were satisfied that the only person who had been with her prior to her death was Parker.'

'You found, I am sure, that her reputation as a gentleman's lady was recognized by her friends. I am assuming that a certain rather scurrilous magazine is accurate in an article. There was no suggestion that Parker was keeping her in the flat?'

'None whatsoever.'

'Or that he saw her with any degree of frequency. Just occasional weekends, you said?'

'So far as we know.'

'So there was no lover driven to frenzy by the threat of the woman to walk out on him for another man. How odd that the defence should not ask why he killed. What did the police suggest was his motive, Sir Edward?'

'We did not suggest any motive, Professor. Where there is an obvious motive it is sometimes referred to. But we do not have to show motive. That is the law. A motive is not a fact of murder; it is a suggestion that exists in the murderer's mind. The police deal only with proven facts. We considered that the facts we had pointed to Parker. It was for the defence to show that they did not.'

'So. L-let us r-regard for a m-moment the p-person of Mrs. Parker.' (The professor had come again to his stammer). 'She d-did not g-give evidence but we h-have it from a w-witness that she s-suspected her h-husband of being unfaithful to her. The witness, Mrs. Walters, heard from Miss Bloss herself that Mrs. Parker had consulted her about trying to get a divorce. Doubtless the police questioned Mrs. Parker although they did not call her?'

'She confirmed that she suspected but had no idea that Miss Bloss was t-the woman. She said she c-consulted her as her life-long friend.'

'That w-was — when?'

'After the arrest of Parker — when she was told the charge.'

'Ah!' The professor wriggled his hands. He took two quick pinches of snuff, and forgot, for once, to brush the grains from his jacket.

'W-would you say t-that Parker w-was a fool?' he asked. 'Or a man of intelligence and acumen?'

'As to that I wouldn't know, Professor. He apparently founded his business and ran it until he took Morley into partnership.'

'So! I s-should h-have imagined from the trial and the defence that he was only a little less a half-wit than his solicitors and counsel.'

He sat back in his chair and searched the faces of the Dilettantes. Deliberately he produced his snuff box and took two pinches. In his old-fashioned dress-jacket turned rusty from age, his dicky-front, overtopped by the big head and his shock of goblin-like grey hair, he looked more than usually out of place in the company sartorially exquisite, and socially impeccable.

For a full minute he occupied himself with his snuff, his wine and his appearance. Then he sat back, spread his hands and leaned forward.

'Well, gentlemen, the evidence is complete,' he said. 'Now I will tell you how Mary Bloss was murdered.' He seemed to the men to be preening himself.

24

'THE incunabula of this disastrous affair is the woman Parker,' the professor began. He looked up with a grimace; and the Dilettantes startled; he had not before been seen to grimace.

'She is a-also t-the eschatology. W-with what unerring rapidity do the suspicions of a w-woman once aroused, identify a target and w-with what uncanny accuracy does her instinct hit it. Her h-husband was c-coming back from h-his hunting without moths — after months of considerable h-hauls of moths. You and I, gentlemen, knowing how collections are amassed and classified and catalogued might have concluded that Parker had been unable to find any new specimens of *lepidoptera*— and did not want to be encumbered with more of the specimens he already had. But not so with an illogical woman. She must jump to the conclusion that there was a more compelling interest. She was right!'

The chairman chuckled. 'So logical conclusions can on occasions be wrong, Professor,' he said.

'W-when it is b-based on assumption, certainly. But not w-when t-the foundation for it is ascertainable fact. I c-continue, yes? Mrs. Parker confided in Mary Bloss; and why not? Who better able to advise her t-than her g-girlhood friend, a b-bridesmaid at her wedding? And what does Miss Bloss say? She asks — and you can imagine in what trepidation — if she knows the w-woman: and the answer is no. But she will seek divorce on account of an unknown woman. Miss Bloss g-gives her the sought-after advice. All husbands she says, g-go off the r-rails now and then. It w-will not last long; you have no evidence; even for an unknown woman you must be able to produce evidence of adultery. Leave the thing alone and it will come to an end.'

The professor smiled, reminiscently. 'As it w-would have d-done,' he said. 'I, who h-have k-known women, tell you that. Now, w-we arrive at the w-weekend of tragedy. On t-this Saturday morning Parker sets off w-with the woman Bloss. She is n-not, mark you, his *inamorata*, but an *affaire s'amuser*; a woman who lives luxuriously, with no income but many men friends. He has no hold on her, n-nor she on h-him. Mrs. Parker has said nothing of her suspicions to her husband, has given h-him no hint; he has no knowledge t-that she views with jealous anger his m-moth-hunting trips. *So why, gentlemen, d-does he p-plot the death of this w-woman: and accomplish it?* That is w-what the C-Crown alleged; and w-what they induced a jury to accept.

The professor thumped the table. 'Why? Why? Why?' His voice rose in indignation. He ceased speaking and sniffed viciously from his snuff. He struggled frantically at a pocket as three loud sneezes registered his nose's protest at the outrage. 'I b-beg your p-pardon,' he apologized. He resumed and his voice sank low and sarcasm tinged it unpleasantly. 'But w-we will be fair,' he said. 'We w-will permit the p-premise that he intended to k-kill; this man whose astuteness and intelligence is s-such that he has founded and b-built up a p-prosperous business. Oh! Oh! he drives t-the w-woman he p-plans to murder in h-his car to a p-place where they have b-been on p-previous occasions — in a car w-which can be t-traced to him by its index number. He k-kills with cyanide, which he is known to possess, and which is even in his car in killing bottles. And he does this, w-when he and only he, is with her except at the fatal moment. Had he advertised, p-publicly his intentions, gentlemen, he c-could not have d-done better. Yes, Sir Edward?'

The Assistant Commissioner had held up a hand trying to get in with a word. He now succeeded. 'I should point out. Professor,' he said, 'that for every premeditated murder, there are four which are unpremeditated. There was, you remember, a quarrel on the Sunday night. It must have some point, as the prosecution insisted.'

'Parker denied any q-quarrel, did he not. He insisted that t-they had only an argument. She wanted to catch moths for the look of the thing and he didn't.'

The A.C. nodded.

'Let us look at t-the w-words overheard in the q-quarrel,' the professor went on. "Why don't you c-catch some moths, you bloody fool . . . Get out and d-don't let me see you until the morning?' W-what is the p-portent of that q-quarrel? Here is the w-woman Bloss *confidante* of the man's wife, and of her suspicions of another woman, because he c-comes back without moths. To-morrow they r-return to Ealing, he once more w-without moths: and his wife's suspicions are strengthened again. The woman says 'Go and get some moths, you bloody fool and allay her suspicions.' Is t-that unlikely? Is it a m-murderous q-quarrel . . .' He paused as a knock at the door was followed by the appearance of a waiter, who handed an envelope to the Assistant Commissioner. Sir Edward slit it open, extracted a sheet of paper which he placed on the table. 'Sorry, Professor,' he apologized. 'Please to continue.'

'Now we are in London' (the professor resumed). 'Parker draws up at t-the flats. Miss Bloss s-steps out and at once the man roars off: he is late. The p-porter sees the arrival. At his h-home Parker's partner is waiting — fuming in anger. 'Blasted moths,' he says. 'We h-have to go to Bedford. Come on.' Mrs. Parker joins in the p-plea: 'I'll put the c-car away and take your things into the house. You get off quickly.' Within five minutes of his arrival he and his partner are off.

'And in the flat, g-gentlemen w-what is Miss Bloss doing? She is m-making a telephone call. Within minutes. S-she has not had time even to t-take off her outdoor clothes, and use her powder puff. She m-must t-telephone, and at once.'

The professor lifted his glass, passed it under his nose for the bouquet and sipped its contents. He turned his eyes on the A.C. 'It is t-time for you to t-tell me w-what the switchboard girl overheard, Sir Edward,' he said. 'They listen, these girls. No. Wait! She c-could n-not recall for you the number. But I, Marcus Stubbs, can t-tell you to w-whom she spoke.' There was a pause, and the Dilet-tantes sensed drama amidst them. They leaned forward.

'*She spoke to Mrs. Parker,*' the professor said.

The A.C. stiffened in his chair. His eyes, on the face of the little man, narrowed.

'Yes?' the professor asked.

Slowly, and with his brows furrowed, the A.C. inclined his head.

'Yes,' he said.

'And w-what was overheard?'

'Not much.' The A.C. picked up from the table the paper that had come to him via the waiter. 'I could not recall with exactitude, the words,' he said, 'so I sent to my office for a copy.' He read out:

> '*I listened to hear the connection was prop-erly made. Miss Bloss said: 'Eileen? This is Mary. Is the old man back from his jaunt? Oh, I see.' The girl said that she was engaged for a few moments with another call. When she returned to see if the conversation had ended, she heard: 'Oh! You mustn't do that by yourself. I'll help.' There was another break. Then — 'Oh, a quarter of an hour.' The girl said she heard no more as she was busy connecting callers.*

That's all,' the A.C. said, and screwed-up the paper. 'It seemed pretty innocuous.'

The professor stared, nodding his head as though in agreement with something. 'The s-solicitors, t-they knew of this?' he asked.

'Parker's? Yes, it was in the depositions.'

'*Cochons! D'alienes!*' The professor exploded. 'That w-which the g-gods give! It w-was in front of their eyes.

I — even, I, not skilled in examination — and who did not k-know w-what was said, saw it.'

'Saw what, Professor?' The psychiatrist, Charles, asked.

'Later! Later! We m-must get on. The d-detectives have finished. They k-know about Hickling, the moths. They have examined t-the equipment, and h-have the cyanide k-killing bottles. Parker is arrested, and his w-wife told. And she is shocked. She d-did not k-know, she said, about Mary Bloss. That is c-correct, Sir Edward?'

'Yes. She said she knew there was a woman, but not that the woman was Bloss.'

'Yet, Sir Edward' — the voice was quiet, and the words came sibilantly — 'yet when Parker's car was examined by Inspector Kenway before the arrest, and a r-rug was found in the back, *Mrs. Parker said it belonged to Mary Bloss.*'

'That is true,' the A.C. said: and stopped. After a pause: 'It is —'

'Odd? Very! *How did Mrs. Parker k-know t-that a rug, with no n-name and no identification, belonged to Miss Bloss?*' He tittered. 'It is a p-problem for d-deduction, gentlemen. Let us deduce. We have certain ascertained f-facts: an urgent telephone call: a car waiting: a wife who will unpack its c-contents . . .' He leaned back in his chair, his eyes looking through and beyond the Dilettantes. His hands went to a waistcoat pocket and withdrew his snuff box. Without glancing at it, he opened the lid and took a pinch from the contents: and restored the box to the pocket. He sniffed and settled down comfortably again in his chair.

'Let us t-take a journey,' he said. 'We are standing with Mrs. Parker in the drive of the house in Ealing. The c-car with the partners is disappearing on its w-way to Bedford. Mrs. Parker has a task to p-perform. She steps into her husband's c-car and drives it into the garage. Now, it must be unpacked. From the b-back she l-lifts out the heavy moth net, the arc-light equipment, and carries them to the house. And she r-returns. T-there are her husband's waterproofs, his rubber thigh boots; they, too, go to the house. She returns a third time — and there is a rug. She lifts out the rug — and t-there on the floor of the car, *she sees something else —*'

The Dilettantes sat silent, hanging on his words and waiting for the strange little man to break the pause which had stilled his telling.

'*She sees a woman's night-case.* For a moment she stares at it, and then a smile, a nasty smile, disfigures her face. She carries the case into the house. 'Now, I shall *know* the woman,' she says: and springs the locks.

'*And there, gentlemen, inside are letters addressed to Mary Bloss.* Now, you realize how she knew to tell Inspector Kenway that the rug belonged to Bloss.

'Picture in your minds the s-scene. She s-stares at the case and anger surges into r-rage, and r-rage into fury. 'Mary,' she says. 'My own friend. I confided in her.' She remembers their talks. 'She was t-the one who s-said I had no evidence — to let things alone . . . I couldn't get a d-divorce . . . laughing at me all the t-time up her sleeve.' And her fury, it is growing.

'And, then, the telephone rings . . . *Mary Bloss has missed within a few minutes, her case left in the car after the blinding rush home because Parker was hours late for his office.* B-but all may be w-well. Perhaps he d-drove straight t-to his office. Perhaps he may even now be at home unpacking the car, and would hide the case. She must find out. She telephones: 'Eileen? Mary here. Is the old man back?'

'Mrs. Parker plays with her. 'Yes, but he's had to go off again. Hadn't t-time to p-put the car away. I'm going to unpack it for him!' And t-then the w-woman Bloss: 'Oh, you mustn't do that by yourself. All t-those heavy things. I'll help you . . . In a quarter of an hour.'

'Mrs. Parker's fury is fanned. The insolence of it. 'I'll get even with her, if it's the l-last t-thing I do,' she says. Suddenly by her hand, she sees the cyanide bottles. She knows all about them and cyanide: she used to help her h-husband w-with the moth-hunting at first, you remember.'

The professor suddenly halted his dramatics. His voice sank to conversational level. 'What man would think of p-poisoning dental cream?' he asked: and there was scorn in his voice. 'Tablets, chocolates, maybe. But d-dental cream is a w-woman's morning and evening habit — as natural to her as t-the use of a c-compact, and cosmetic creams. Into the t-tube of cream Mrs. Parker lets fall drop after drop . . . after drop . . . of t-the cyanide, and replaces the cap. She puts it b-back into the c-case and c-carries the case back to t-the c-car and covers it again w-with the rug. She t-takes back the other t-things. And then she w-waits.

'And Mary Bloss comes — oh, yes, I know she w-was n-not seen to leave the flat after the morning return. W-was the p-porter, then, sitting in the doorway, with no absences to answer c-calls from flats, from tradesmen, and so on? Mary Bloss comes with her false friend's smile. 'We will clear the c-car,' she says, 'and then have a cup of tea.' She finds the c-car still p-packed. Oh, Fortune! She helps with t-the unloading. With Mrs. Parker's back turned towards t-the house, she retrieves her case, and conceals it — in the garage, by the hedge, in the front porch — where d-does it m-matter. And w-when she leaves, she c-carries it w-with her. Do you d-doubt that Mrs. Parker from a window, watched her w-walk away with it?

'And at bedtime Mary Bloss c-cleans her teeth — and goes to her last s-sleep. Well was it said by Congreve that

Heaven has no rage like love to hatred t-turned, nor Hell a fury like a w-woman scorned. Eileen Parker had rid herself of Mary Bloss, and — because of the fatuousness of his defence — of her faithless husband, too.'

He turned and faced the A.C. who was sitting, agitated in his chair.

'B-but all is not yet lost, Sir Edward,' he said. 'Ask the w-woman, without dissemblance, w-what she d-did with Mary Bloss's case which she f-found in t-the c-car. The answer w-will be in her face.'

He rose, and with a little, old-fashioned, bow to the company walked slowly to the door, and through it.

25

THE bizarre episodes which the newspapers came to call 'The Strange Case of the Sleepers' occurred during the hot months of July and August: England being the fortunate recipient of a summer in that year. Up to the second week in September they were still unsolved. On the fourteenth of September the Dilettantes met for the first time after the club's August recess. The subject for their discussion had been chosen by the chairman, Sir Noël Maurice, 'Perception'; and each member had been thus informed by letter-card.

Unfortunately, the debate seemed likely to fall below the usual keen controversial level: there was an unfortunate quality of agreement — of view. As befitted his calling as a psychiatrist Norman Charles propounded the problem, and in doing so, arrayed perception against induction. He illustrated the point. 'The phenomenon of perception,' he maintained, 'is clearly shown in panoramas. The principal trick in these consists in putting in the foreground real objects (stones, trunks of trees, wheels, etc.) which become to all appearances part of the picture. The eye of the spectator is attracted to these objects, is convinced by their materiality, and immediately transfers his impression to the portion that is only paint and canvas so successfully that the whole appears real. This inductive faculty,' he maintained, 'is of first importance in the study of Perception.'

Alexander Purcell, the mathematician, supported him. 'I agree, Charles,' he said. 'Let us emphasize it with still more examples — or should I say illusions. If, a little before rain falls, mountains appear nearer, it is not because the eye is deceived, but because in calculating the distance we have forgotten that air charged with humidity refracts the light. In the same way if a stick is held slanting in water, refraction makes the portion submerged in the water appear to be raised up, so as to form an obtuse angle with the other portion. There is no error in the senses, for if the stick should be photographed it will appear in the photograph also broken in an obtuse angle. There will be no mistake unless we believe that the stick is really broken.'

The professor entered into the argument. 'Ah, that is the p-point,' he said. 'T-that is the p-point.' He was leaning forward and seemed in a state of excitement. 'Now, y-you t-trespass on my p-provinces — the p-provinces of logic and psychology, gentlemen. I will g-give you even more odd examples of perception and induction. A line with d-divisions appears shorter than a continuous line. A square d-divided by a d-diagonal appears broader than high, while a square divided by a v-vertical appears h-higher t-than it is broad. Vertical lines cut across by short oblique parallel lines appear to d-diverge from t-the vertical in t-the d-direction opposite to t-that of the c-cutting lines.' He chuckled. 'Indeed I know. I have t-taken many pounds from my students at Bonn by betting with them. They wagered on P-perception.' He laughed delightedly, and then snorted.

'B-but we must not jest on s-such a s-subject. These illusions, t-they can exercise a decisive influence on t-the d-depositions of witnesses, and t-the g-grossest mistakes may slip into an inquiry if we simply accept the depositions of such perception!'

The professor looked up, he shook his goblin-like shock of hair. 'It is, I think, illustrated by circumstances very much in the news at t-the m-moment.'

'That being, Professor?' the chairman asked, as the professor paused, invitingly.

'In t-the peculiar — t-the very p-peculiar — story of the sleeping robberies.' He turned to the Assistant Commissioner, and bowed.

Sir Edward Allen drew his eyebrows together, and considered the point, carefully — and unsuccessfully. 'You go beyond me, Professor,' he said. 'I do not follow the line of argument.'

'Y-yet it is simple, Sir Edward. All the p-persons were robbed in a matter of seconds, is it not? That is what we have read in the newspapers. Three of the f-four people saw a p-person and spoke to him. Each says q-quite distinctly that s-such p-person carried out no operation of any kind, d-did nothing to them. Yet t-that p-person in each case m-must have been the r-robber. Is it so?'

The A.C. nodded. 'There was no other contact. Professor.'

'So! Then their p-perception is at fault. And their description of the incidents; they, too, are false. Their testimony is induction based on what they think did *not* happen. And so the police have lost a clue t-that is somewhere hovering around. Until the induction is put aside and deduction from perception is p-promoted in its place t-the m-mystery must remain.'

The A.C. frowned. 'That there is a clue somewhere is certain,' he said. 'But as to the robberies, the robberies, as I have said occupied only two or three seconds —'

'Sir Edward, t-the eye c-can see in a ten thousandth part of a second and p-photograph to the brain what it has seen. This the eyes of the victims did in all t-the c-cases. Something was seen. There was perception —'

The chairman interposed. 'The debate has taken an unexpected turn, Edward,' he chortled. 'Shall we now debate with the professor what it could be that was perceived?'

A chorus of assent greeted the suggestion. Sir Edward smiled. 'I will play my part, Noël. There are one or two points which have not been disclosed to the Press or public.'

'Then, after we have replenished our glasses and our cigars we will hear them.'

* * *

'Well, now,' the A.C. began, 'the story starts with a Mister Silas Abrahams, who is a money-lender. He has a two-roomed office in Angel Street, Limehouse. The office is on the ground floor of a rather old block — or rather a large Victorian house split up into business premises.

'At eleven o'clock on July 3rd, Abrahams went to his bank and drew out £200 in notes on a cheque. Back in his office Abrahams placed the money in a steel cash-box, which he locked and put in a drawer of his desk.

'I should, perhaps, have explained the lay-out of the office. Abraham's room is on the front with a window overlooking the main street, and another, smaller one overlooking a side turning. Behind his room is another room occupied by his clerk, and giving on to the front room through a door. There is no entry to Abraham's room except through this inner door. A doorway which at one time opened direct into the hall, or passage, was blocked up when Abrahams rented the premises some years ago. The door of the clerk's room opens into the hall. That is the only entrance to the office.

'Between 11.20, when he returned from the bank, and midday Abrahams was busy with papers and his accounts at his desk. At midday his clerk, an elderly man named Jacobs, put his head round the inside door and announced that he was going to lunch — that being his customary time. And to lunch he went, closing the outer door behind him. Abrahams, he said, at that time was still busy at his desk — and was quite well.

'He returned from lunch at 12.45, and opened the door. Now this outside door was fitted with a warning signal; when it was opened either from outside or inside a bell rang continuously until the door was closed again. It was the practice of Abrahams when the bell rang to call out, 'Who is it?' whether the clerk was in the outer room or not. On this occasion, hearing no such demand, Jacobs opened the inner door and looked in to see whether his employer had gone out. He saw him lying with his head on his arms on the desk, apparently asleep. He went across and shook him, calling out some such remark as 'It's nearly 1 o'clock, sir.' Abrahams did not move. Becoming alarmed Jacobs ran into the street and called a policeman who was on point duty a few yards away. Hardly had the constable entered the room than Abrahams sat up. He looked from his clerk to the constable, and said: 'What the hell's going on here? What's he doing?' pointing to the police. The clerk explained the circumstances, and the constable, reporting later, said Abraham's face was a picture of amazement. He said: 'Nonsense, man, there's nothing the matter with me.

Get out.' Later, both Jacobs and the constable agreed that he was alert, and in full possession of his faculties. This is important in view of subsequent happenings.

'Now, at this moment the bell signalled the entry of someone in the outside room. Jacobs went out, to return immediately with the news that an expected client had arrived. He was ushered in and Jacobs retired to the outer room with the constable, who pulled out a notebook and prepared to enter an account of the visit. He had hardly wetted the point of his pencil (which is a preliminary with all constables — why I'm hanged if I know!) when there was a shout from the inside room. The door flew open and Abrahams appeared in the opening. 'The money,' he shouted. 'The money. God, it's gone'; and proceeded to weep and wail.

'The constable, a quick-witted man, with a shout of 'Don't touch anything,' headed the company, including the client, into the outer room, and telephoned the C.I.D. To Detective-Sergeant Player, Jacobs told his story. Then, when he had sufficiently recovered from his shock, Abrahams told his.'

26

'A VERY odd story it was,' Sir Edward paused and took a sip from Moroni's 1927 Port, which is guarded in the cellars as jealously as the gold in Fort Knox — and is pretty nearly as valuable. He knocked a length of ash from his cigar — and proceeded.

'He said he was writing at his desk when he suddenly went all queer. The next thing he remembered was seeing the constable and his clerk looking down at him. Pressed at what time he came over queer, he said it must have been shortly after 12.15 because he remembered checking his watch by the quarter-hour chime of the clock of the church across the road. He had seen nobody, and heard nothing; and he had had no callers up to his passing out.'

The A.C. looked round at his fellow Dilettantes and grimaced. 'Now we went into this fantastic story very thoroughly,' he said. 'And I'll tell you why: Abrahams is a very shady character. He has been under suspicion by us for a long time. He had been involved in an attempted fraud in which a considerable sum of money was involved. He was never prosecuted because the complainant suddenly with-drew his allegations. Said it was a mistake. We found that Abrahams was insured against theft; and our first idea was, in view of the circumstances we *didn't* find, that there had never been any theft but that he would collect from the insurance company the £200 said to have been stolen —'

'What circumstances didn't you find, Edward?' the chairman asked.

'Material evidence, Noël. There were no traces of any forced entry. Although Prints went over every inch of the office, the only finger prints they found were those of Abrahams and Jacobs, and two of the client who, when he sat down in the chair, had put his hands on the arms.'

'Gloves, A.C.?' queried James, the pathologist.

'Usually a gloved hand leave smears: we found none. We thought the man might have taken something to put himself out temporarily and make it appear as though he had been drugged, so we called in the police doctor. Abrahams gave no reaction to tests; the doctor said he appeared quite normal.'

'Gassed, perhaps?' Charles suggested. The A.C. smiled. 'He would have shown signs as James, there, knows. He didn't. I said that the doctor and Jacobs earlier said he appeared quite normal — no sleepiness or drowsiness when he came to. Anyway the laboratory lads tested the room for all the usual gases and found nothing.'

'W-who knew he h-had the £200?' the professor asked.

'He did, and Jacobs did. The client probably expected it would be there. Beyond that — nobody.'

'The client may have come a little earlier and purloined it — and then turned up at the arranged time as an alibi?' Sir Noël Maurice made the suggestion.

'Then, how did he get in the office, Noël?' the A.C. said. 'Remember the warning bell. However we went into that. The man is perfectly respectable, and in a good way of business, but wanted the loan of £200 for a few weeks. The same can be said for Jacobs the clerk. He is an honest person.'

There was a hiatus of silence while the Dilettantes chewed the cud over the evidence produced by the A.C. It was broken by the professor. 'You say there were no signs of forcible entry. That is by the door, I presume. W-what about the w-windows? Were they open; it was a hot day I think.'

'One was open about three inches at the bottom, Professor. The other, on the main street, was screwed up.' He held up a hand as the professor was about to speak. 'That cock won't fight. The open window could not be opened any further. It had jammed. Well, there it is,' he concluded. 'We spent a week on the case —'

'Did the insurance company pay out?' the chairman asked.

'Yes. They had no option. Candidly, our people were of the firm opinion that Abrahams had worked another trick, but we had nothing to prove it. We ceased to have any further interest in the affair.'

Sir Edward drew on his cigar, and expelled the smoke between his lips in a series of smoke rings, stabbing each one through with a finger as it ascended. He directed a rather wry smile at the company as he spoke again. 'Then there occurred something which knocked our idea for six,' he said.

'The second incident occurred, eh?' the chairman said.

'It did —'

The chairman interposed. 'Before the second instalment, I suggest we give Sir Edward a breathing space, and have a supply of Moroni's Russian coffee.' The proposal met with approval, and it was not until a quarter of an hour later that the A.C. continued with the second episode of his bizarre story. He waited until the professor had dusted from his lapels the grains of brown left by a copious inhalation of snuff from his silver snuff-box.

'It happened a fortnight later,' the A.C. said. 'Shortlands were holding a *salon* in the Splendide Hotel. I don't need to tell you — with perhaps the exception of the professor — that Shortlands is the premier Fashion House in Britain; our wives are extravagant worshippers at the shrine.'

Sir Noël Maurice laughed. 'That is so in my case, Edward.'

'And in mine,' Charles agreed.

'And mine,' Sir Edward said. 'The display was to begin at 3 o'clock in the grand *salon* of the hotel. Some half a dozen models were to present the frocks. Shortlands principal model is a honey-blonde called Adèle Narraway. Now, Adèle is a girl with a streak of business acumen in her, and an eye to the main chance. She had a business arrangement with Lartiers, the jewel house, whereby when she was modelling for Shortlands, she wore jewellery from Lartiers — and the fact was advertised discreetly at the dress shows. In other words, she set off the frocks with exquisite jewels, and set off the jewels with exquisite frocks: which brought her two modelling fees for one job.

'She was due to arrive at the Splendide at 2.15 o'clock for the parade beginning at 3 o'clock. She left her flat in Chelsea at 1.45, driving herself in her own small saloon car. She wended her slow way to Lartiers, in Bond Street, and there was shown into the manager's room. Adèle has said that there was a discussion over what jewellery she should show. After describing the frocks she was to model, the manager was of the opinion that pearls would be the best set-off for the frocks, especially as pearls were decidedly *à la mode* at the moment. Together they chose four necklaces, with ear-rings to match. The collection was valued at more than £6,000, and over the telephone the manager effected the necessary insurance covering the time the pearls left the shop until they were returned. The pearls were placed in a case, which Adèle put into her own dressing-case, which contained her cosmetics etc. It was the case she always carried when she modelled.'

The chairman interrupted. 'Just a moment, Edward. 'Was this the usual procedure? It seems rather a haphazard way of dealing with valuable jewellery.'

'That, of course, Lartiers know now, and the jewels in future will be taken to the shows by one of the firm guarded by a detective. But up to this occasion Miss Narraway had followed the procedure many times without untoward results. To continue the story: She left Lartiers at 2 o'clock and drove along to the Splendide. It was as she was about to drive into the courtyard that the incident occurred. A large car was endeavouring to turn at the entrance and this blocked the way for a minute or so. Seeing Miss Narraway waiting, the driver got out and approached her car, opened the door on the near side and with a smile apologized for the delay. Then he raised his hat, closed the door, went back to his own car, and after straightening the steering, drove away —'

'Is he k-known?' the professor asked. The A.C. smiled.

'No,' he said. 'Our inquiries revealed that he had never been inside the courtyard, but was parked alongside the pavement and moved only, we assume, when Adèle's car came along. Anyway, Adèle waited until his car had left, a matter of a minute and then drove in. One or two cars were at the hotel entrance picking up departing clients and it was some three minutes or more before the commissionaire motioned her up to the door. She did not move and seemed to be lolling over the wheel. A man stepped forward from the hotel steps, looked in the window and then opened the door. He shouted to the commissionaire: 'The lady seems to be ill.' The commissionaire and two porters crowded at the door. Adèle was half-sitting, half-lying in the driver's seat. She was carried unconscious into the hotel lounge and a doctor was called. But it was nearly half an hour before she came round. Not until then was her dressing-case — and the jewels — missed.' The A.C. looked round. 'Now, what do you make of that?' he asked.

'T-the m-man who w-went to her a-assistance, what d-does he say?' the professor asked.

'We would very much like to know.' The A.C. smiled grimly. 'However, we can't find him. He just walked away in the confusion. To continue: Adèle, half-hysterical, told her story to the hotel detective. An old C.I.D. man and alert, he telephoned straight through to Scotland Yard. Inspector Kenway went at once. What he heard he told to Superintendent Jones and myself — and we revised the opinions we had held about Abrahams.'

'What *was* her story?' Charles asked.

'That she had suddenly, and unaccountably come over all queer, and the next she knew was finding herself on a hotel lounge with a doctor bending over her. It coincided exactly with the sensations of Abrahams. The case, she said, had been on the vacant seat beside her when she drove into the courtyard, and was there, she says, when she began to feel queer.'

'And then?' the chairman queried.

'We had her car towed to Scotland Yard and we turned it inside out in examination. Gassing was first thought of, of course. The carpet was tested, with litmus paper, and so on: there was no reaction of any kind.'

'And Adèle?' James asked.

'The doctor, and our own police doctor — could find no explanation whatever for her illness. When she recovered consciousness she was normal in every way except for hysterics. There was nothing whatever wrong with her any more than there had been with Abrahams.'

27

'You were completely fogged,' Charles suggested.

'Completely,' the A.C. agreed. 'Once we had disposed of gassing in some shape or form and, as I have said, we got no reaction to gas, we were entirely without a clue. The laboratory can solve most riddles if it has something to work on, but in this case there was nothing for it to get into.'

'Did you try for sulphur?' James, the pathologist, asked.

'Sulphur?' The A.C. looked at him, surprised. 'Why sulphur?'

'Mephistopheles. He wouldn't leave any trace same as when he appeared and disappeared in 'Faust'.'

The A.C. grinned. 'And what would Mephistopheles want with £6,000 worth of pearls and £200 in notes?' He took another cigar removed the band and pierced it with a silver cutter; and then sat back in his chair and lit it. A connoisseur in cigars he expelled the smoke from the lighting after he had removed the cigar from his mouth: smoke should never be blown into a cigar. The professor, too sat back in his chair, relaxed. He produced his snuff box and took two pinches. Afterwards he flicked with a silk handkerchief the left traces of brown dust which had been deposited on what was obviously a "dicky' shirt-front, repeating the action on the lapels of his aged and shining dinner jacket. The chairman passed the port round and they refilled their glasses.

James restarted the narrative. "You intrigue me as a pathologist, A.C.' he said. "What do you know about Adèle? Is she, for instance given to occasional depression? Is she at times irritable?'

"Meaning?'

"Well, I was thinking of functional trouble of the heart, which could affect its mechanism — the control of the different cavities. It could lead to fainting fits or black-outs.' The A.C. nodded. 'Our surgeon had the same idea,' he said. 'And disproved the theory. The heart action of both Adèle and Abrahams were absolutely normal.'

'Well, Edward, your people have missed something, somewhere,' the chairman decided. 'Facts are facts. Nobody can walk about places, knock people out and leave no sign of any kind behind him. Even Marley's ghost left a sound of clanging chains.'

'As against James's idea,' Charles said, 'it would be a remarkable coincidence if two people suddenly had a functional disorder of the heart at the very moment that somebody strolled up with the purpose of despoiling them of money and jewels.'

The A.C. grinned. 'And still more so, Charles, if the same thing happened to a third person in similar circumstances.'

'Ah! the third case,' the chairman said.

'Indeed! The third sleeper was Mr. Joshua Hemingway, a diamond expert in Hatton Garden, and probably the best designer and re-setter of jewellery in Britain,' the A.C. said. 'Now, whatever evil suspicions we might have entertained regarding Abrahams, there were none felt regarding Hemingway. He is a most respected member of society —'

'So was Doctor Crippen,' Charles said.

'— whose integrity is beyond question. At 4 o'clock in the afternoon, three weeks to the day after the Splendide affair, he telephoned the Garden police-station in a state of great excitement. He was only half-coherent, but was understood to say that he had been robbed of an article of great value. A sergeant went round, and hearing Hemingway's story, a tale now becoming unpleasantly familiar to the London police, promptly sat the man in a corner of his room, told him not to touch anything and telephoned Scotland Yard. Inspector Kenway hurried round,' the A.C. paused.

'Tell me the old, old story!' The A.C. hummed the first line of the hymn and the Dilettantes smiled.

'Quite!' the A.C. agreed. 'Kenway found the sergeant and Hemingway still in the room — which was, in fact, a workshop, if rather a superior kind of workshop. I can describe the room to you, since I visited it myself. It was about 20 feet by 18. Down the centre ran a long table, or bench, some 9 feet by 6 feet with, on it, a lathe and various other mechanical equipment. A high back ran along one side and this was composed of drawers, similar to those you see behind the counter of a chemist's shop. At the base of this back were hanging in loops various jeweller's tools. A pair of jeweller's scales were in front of them. In the front centre of the table was a large square of black velvet. The room had a large window which was a quarter open at the top. The door was in a corner of the room. Over the bench was a large but softened cluster of electric bulbs.'

The A.C. halted to draw on his cigar, which had burned unevenly. He waited until it drew level again, and then flicked off the ash. The end glowed under the softly dim lights of the club room. He looked round the waiting Dilettantes. 'The valuable article which had gone was a £3,000 diamond necklace. Hemingway said he was cleaning the stones and re-setting the necklace for Burtrams, the West End jewellers on behalf of a titled client. He had started the work in the morning, and stopped for lunch at 1 o'clock locking the necklace in his safe. He returned at 2 o'clock, took out the necklace and loose stones, locking the safe again — his usual precautionary practice because there were many valuables in it. This probably saved him from an even greater loss.

'Then, he says, he sat down at his bench and began work again. The necklace and the loose stones were in front of him on the velvet square. At 2.30 o'clock — he knows it was 2.30 because he had only a moment before looked at his watch as he was expecting a telephone call — he says he suddenly came over all queer. His head was spinning round, and he had to put his tools down. That was the last thing he remembered until shortly after 3 o'clock he — as he says — 'woke up'. There were no diamonds on his bench, but he was not then worried about that; he assumed that he had put them in the safe when he thought he was going to sleep. He found out his mistake when he went to the safe to get them. Then he thought back and remembered his spinning head, etc.

'As I say, Kenway went to his room. And with the other sleepers in view he went prepared with a laboratory man. The lab. had the idea that in the other cases they were not called until some time after the happening, when fumes of some sort might have been dissipated. The officers laid on the floor and smelled with delicate noses; they tried every known agent for gases, fumes and so on. And they found nothing. Hemingway was in a pretty distressed state; but because of shock, and not in health. He was sound in every way. And that is as far as our people have got.'

'And there were no indications of any kind in the room?' Charles asked.

'Not a sign of anything. No fingerprints and no glove smears. And I will forestall you by saying there was no evidence of anything having been wiped clean.'

'The window again?' asked James.

'Permanently screwed down at the bottom half; the top was as I have said, open a third of the way down. And the street outside is a busy one: even a half-wit seeing anybody climbing over a window would have raised an alarm. In point of fact, a newspaper seller was standing on his pitch a few feet away: he saw no intruder getting in or out.'

'Who knew Hemingway was working on the necklace?' the chairman asked.

'Burtrams knew, because the director had commissioned Hemingway to do the work.'

'And, of course, the assistants — or at least some of them?'

'Yes. It was an assistant who took the necklace to his workshop.'

'And the people in Lartiers knew of the pearls Miss Narraway would be carrying,' the chairman said significantly.

'Nobody was missing from the firms at the time of the robberies,' the A.C. replied. 'We, of course, saw the possibility.'

28

Sir Edward Allen finished a cup of coffee which had been called for by the chairman, and looked at his watch. 'Time is getting on if we are to have the usual discussion,' he said. 'So I will hurry over the last case.

'It concerns a Mr. Wilfred Gibbs, who is a manufacturing chemist in Wardour Street, W. At 6.10 one morning a police patrol car trundling along Western Avenue, near Ealing Golf Club entrance came on a car with two wheels on the road and the front wheels over the grass verge and resting on the pavement. Inside, Gibbs was apparently asleep. Since motorists, even at 6.10 a.m., are not supposed to sleep at the wheel of a car straddling its rear end in the roadway the police driver pulled up to remonstrate. His words apparently falling on deaf ears he shook the man. This failing again to produce any effect, he pulled him roughly by the shoulder. It was when this failed to rouse Gibbs that he remembered the sleepers. He called the Yard on his radio. Kenway — who was the unfortunate fellow saddled with the sleepers — was hauled out of bed and by the time he had dressed a squad car was waiting for him. Gibbs was still asleep when he reached the spot. He decided on drastic methods. He had the police car tow the car as fast as they could into London and to the Yard, he himself steering.

'At the Yard Gibbs was lifted out and carried to a room, the stretcher used being laid with the ends on a couple of chairs. Our own surgeon examined him. He was breathing normally, his pulse even. His eyes, when the lids were lifted, showed neither dilation nor contraction. There was no smell of alcohol about him. Examination of the car produced the usual result — nothing.'

The A.C. smiled broadly. 'Well, we sat round him in the sure and certain hope that presently he would wake, and ask where the hell he was.'

'And he did?' James asked.

'He did — in those very words. He opened his eyes, and stared round him. Then, as the strangeness of his surroundings broke into his consciousness, he sat up and used the phrase I've mentioned. Told he was in Scotland Yard, he nearly fainted. Asked if he was feeling all right he replied: 'All right. Yes. I'm feeling all right. Why shouldn't I be. And why am I in Scotland Yard?' Told we would like him to look at his car, he walked round it eyeing it all over. 'Seems O.K. to me,' he said. 'What's supposed to be wrong with it?' Asked if things were all right inside, he opened the door and said 'yes'. Kenway asked, 'Nothing missing?' and Gibbs said 'No,' adding: 'Look, what's going on?'

'Kenway outlined the story of the roadside and the man stared, Kenway says in bewilderment. 'Asleep in the car!' he echoed. 'Well, I'd been driving a good time, I admit. I'd come from Birmingham. But I've done it once a month for a couple of years and never fallen asleep before. It's a queer do to me!'

'Kenway asked whether he could remember anything which may have caused him to lose consciousness. Did he feel faintness coming on. Had he over-tired himself the previous day. He replied that he couldn't remember feeling anything. He didn't remember falling asleep. It was, he declared, a mystery to him. Asked if he had given a lift to a pedestrian he said he never gave lifts to anyone. Then he paused and Kenway alerted. 'Yes?' he invited. Gibbs then said that he *was* stopped once, but that couldn't have had anything to do with his going to sleep. A man on a motorcycle had signalled him to pull up and had then asked if he was right for Oxford. Questioned, he said the man did not get into the car, but opened the rear door on the offside — as Gibbs had run slightly past him. 'He wasn't there more than a quarter of a minute!' Gibbs said. 'I told him to follow the avenue round and he'd strike the main road to Wycombe and Oxford. He thanked me, closed the door and drove off'.'

The A.C. sat back. 'Well, that's the whole story,' he concluded. 'We checked on Gibbs, and he is exactly what he says he is — and is quite well known as a manufacturing chemist in a pretty fair way of business.'

The period of silence during which the Dilettantes mentally digested the details of the A.C.'s tale was broken by a loud chuckle and comment from Purcell. 'Well, I must say it's a rummy business.'

'There is one thing pretty obvious, Edward,' the chairman said when, once again fortified with coffee, they settled down to pros and cons.

'That being?' the A.C. asked.

'That the perpetrators knew of the existence of the stolen property. You say that none of the staff of Lartiers or Burtrams were away from the firms during the time of the robberies, and you exonerate them. *But could there be amongst them an inside man* passing on vital information of the jewellery and the venue?'

'There could be, Noël, but the operator acting on such information could hardly have had time to plan the Splendide affair. Adèle drove straight from Lartiers to the hotel, you know.'

'Oh, yes, he could,' James protested. 'He might not have known exactly what she was carrying, but he knew she would be carrying something valuable. She had been modelling jewellery with the frocks for a year or more. An inside man could be pretty certain in assuming that she would do the same for a show like that at Splendide.

What time did he have to plan a raid? The show had been written about in the fashion journals for a month. You can bet a mink coat to a yard of chiffon that Lartiers had fixed up with Adèle to show something — even if they hadn't decided what.'

'They couldn't decide until Adèle knew for certain what kind of frocks she was to wear,' Purcell pointed out.

'All that was wanted by the operator was to see Adèle leave the shop — and the operation was in progress,' Charles concluded.

The A.C. nodded — and smiled. 'You do not seem to be any less alert in theorizing than the police,' he said. 'But we are unable to produce any evidence of inside information, though there is always the possibility.'

The professor entered the discussion for the first time. He had been listening with obvious interest, for he had taken no snuff, and his hands had never once roamed through the goblin-like shock of hair.

'W-who do you s-suggest robbed Miss Narraway?' he asked. 'The man in the drawn-up car, or he who noticed the w-woman over t-the w-wheel, opened the d-door and shouted 'the lady is ill'?'

The A.C. replied: 'Adèle is certain that the case was in the seat by her side when she drove into the courtyard,' he said. 'So I suppose the man who called out that she appeared to be ill.'

Then who was it made her ill?' The professor chuckled. 'We h-have s-strayed b-back to perception, my friends. Miss Narraway, I doubt she would look at the seat to see whether the case was there: she would be too fully occupied in steering her car into the courtyard past the line of departing vehicles. It is a task r-requiring much concentration, so I am assured by motorists who drive in such c-circumstances. Her perception of the case, I t-think, was in her m-mind's eye. She h-had p-put the case on t-the seat, s-she h-had not t-touched it since. Nobody h-had entered the c-car, and she h-had not left it, until she was carried out. Ergo, the case *m-must* have been on the seat.'

'Then you think it was the man in the car. Professor?'

The odd little man chuckled again. 'I t-think it was b-both of them,' he said. 'In collusion. The m-man in the c-car induced the sleeping. The other man took the c-case, w-when Miss Narraway was in a s-state of unconsciousness. In the confusion the f-fact t-that he took the c-case wouldn't be commented upon.'

Charles broke in. 'I don't think so, Professor,' he said. 'That would suggest an accomplice. There is no evidence of accomplice in either of the other three cases. In fact, so far as Gibbs is concerned, only one person is involved — the motor-cyclist who stopped him.'

The chairman rapped on the table. 'All this is going away from the point, gentlemen — which is what caused the four sleepers to sleep? That is the problem, Edward, is it not?'

The A.C. nodded.

'T-there is one point,' the professor looked round the Dilettantes and paused. 'A point t-that might i-interest Scotland Yard,' he added.

The A.C. looked up. 'Yes?' he invited.

'What was it of which t-the w-worthy Mr. Gibbs was robbed?'

'Eh? He was not robbed, Professor,' the A.C. said. 'He said that nothing was missing.'

'Then w-why was he stopped and s-sent to sleep? T-this sleep-maker d-does not work for l-love, gentlemen. Look at that for which he procured sleep — to relieve the man Abrahams of £200: to p-possess pearls worth £6,000; to obtain diamonds worth £3,000. And from Mr. Gibbs

. . . n-nothing at all. Yet he stops a little manufacturing c-chemist!'

The professor paused. He produced his snuff box and sniffed twice from his fingers; his eyes watched from under his shock of hair and over the lenses of his spectacles perched half-way down his nose.

'He is lying!' he said. 'Since he makes that journey regularly, once a month, it w-would be w-well if he were stopped again, this t-time by Sir Edward's men, to discover w-what he is c-carrying t-that he w-wants so m-much to keep secret.

'As for t-this sleeping, I am a logician. Sir Edward tells us t-there were no clues, no traces. T-there is no logic in that. Formal logic, w-which is t-the first p-part of the formula of logic, is concerned with d-deductive reasoning. And it is not deductive reasoning, nor logical sense to say t-that a m-man commits an offence against the p-person and leaves no trace of himself or his *modus operandi*. Sir Edward has said that examination was m-made of all the p-premises. The car of Mr. Gibbs w-was taken to Scotland Yard and examined. No doubt the m-men of the l-laboratory used the electrical device t-that sucks up t-the dust and the odd things that are hidden in rugs, and carpets. B-but he h-has not said what t-they found. He looked across at the A.C.

'Yes,' the A.C. assented. 'I did not mention it because we found nothing. There was dust, of course, and a small quantity of white powder.' The professor was about to speak, but was halted by a wave of the hand. 'We tested various samples of the powder; it was the same that was in the cricks of his shoes and in his trouser turn-ups — mostly chalk.' He smiled. 'Gibbs makes pills for digestive upsets,' he added. 'There were some fine splinters of thin glass slightly convex-shaped. Gibbs's wristwatch was minus the face glass. He had apparently knocked it against the wheel when he fell forward, asleep. That is all.'

'So!' The professor said, slouched back in his chair, and became silent. The Dilettantes waited a minute. Then: 'Professor,' the chairman reminded him. He came to with a little jerk of his head.

'Oh, yes,' he said; and then he laughed — a high pitched tittering laugh, which ceased abruptly as he caught the glances of his fellow members. 'I make m-my apologies, Mr. Chairman,' he said. 'I w-was carried away. The m-mystery, it is solved. I, Marcus Stubbs, Professor of Logic, know the answer.'

'What is it?' the A.C. asked, and leaned forward.

'I will show you how your sleepers slept,' the professor said. 'Oh, yes, I will show you.' His goblin-like shock of hair shook as he nodded his head. Behind this thick lenses his eyes were twinkling. 'Yes, I will show you' — he looked at his watch. 'But not to-night, for it is 10.30 o'clock, and time for us to leave the club, and it will take some time.' In his enjoyment of the moment he was forgetting to stutter. 'Also, I must think out one or two details. But at the next meeting — you will see.' He looked across at Sir Edward Allen. 'Remember, Sir Edward, what I told you,' he said.

29

IT was with a pleasurable sense of anticipation that the Dilettantes gathered for their next fortnightly dinner. Sir Edward Allen, the Assistant Commissioner (Crime) of Scotland Yard, had spent the intervening time fuming over the delay, and castigating the professor for the display of egoism by which he indulged his fancy for keeping his hearers on tenter-hooks. He was still to simmer for some time, for, according to the rule of the club, no mention of the topic for discussion was permissible until after dinner had been eaten, the table cleared by the ancient and rather tottering waiter, and the liqueurs and coffee brought in, together with the port and nuts to follow.

Moroni had served as the fish course Dover Sole, prepared to his own recipe, and with it *sauce piquant*. The professor, accepting it from the waiter chuckled, and continued to chuckle, almost under his breath. 'It is the sauce,' he said in answer to mute questioning for his merriment. 'Piquant! T-that is very good for to-night.' The wine served was Oviete, an Italian wine of rare softness and bouquet. It was an hour before dinner ended, and the waiter, his duties over, left the Dilettantes to themselves; and the chairman raised the matter for which they were waiting. 'Now, Professor,' he said.

Sir Edward intervened. 'I think I should tell you that this morning, early, we arrested Mr. Gibbs, the chemist, in his car as he reached his shop,' he said. 'He will appear at a special sitting of magistrates to-morrow morning.' He looked across the table. 'Thank you, Professor,' he said.

'W-what was he c-carrying?'

'Heroin. Sold to addicts it would mean more than £2,000 worth.'

'So!' the professor said. 'I thought it might have been cocaine.'

The A.C. looked curiously at him. The professor smiled. 'To a man of logic, Sir Edward, it was of no difficulty. That he was r-robbed was certain from the fact that he was sent to sleep why else s-should he have been thus attacked? His denial made it plain that he had been robbed of something he didn't desire t-to reveal to the p-police. W-what has a manufacturing c-chemist that he d-dare not reveal to the law. There is only one a-answer — drugs. C-cocaine was the most likely. Psh — that is all t-there is t-to it.'

'The sleepers?' Sir Edward asked.

'Ah, the sleepers.' The professor sat back as though seeking how to begin. From his snuff box he took two pinches and settled himself in his chair.

'T-there is one common denominator to all t-the sleepings,' he began. 'All went t-to unconsciousness in a c-confined space. Two in r-rooms and t-two in s-saloon cars. In each c-case there were w-windows which w-were either open, or could be open. H-how were t-they attacked? They w-were not pricked by a hypodermic syringe because the m-method of attack w-was the s-same in all cases; and in the c-case of Abrahams and Hemingway *t-there w-was no access to the victim until after he was unconscious*. Therefore the s-same means which had proved s-successful would h-have been employed in the remaining instances.

'Sir Edward' — he nodded at the A.C. — 'says the police got no reaction to gas. B-but it must be noted that from h-half to three quarters-of-an-hour at least h-had elapsed since any gas had been r-released. It was a b-baffling enigma to me until Sir Edward detailed the findings in the car of the man Gibbs. Then there came t-to me a stirring of the memory —'

'Something I said?' The A.C. wrinkled his brows in an effort to recall the details.

'The mind, it is an incomprehensible thing,' the professor went on. 'It stores away trifles of no moment, as an eccentric miser stores useless bric-à-brac in a lumber room. And t-the t-trifle goes into t-the lumber of unremembered things. Then, suddenly, without reason, t-the trifle comes b-back to mind. Some day I must take up t-the study of mental phenomena,' he added, inconsequentially. 'So it was with the sleepers. To my memory came recollection of many years ago . . . a student in Bonn where I had a Chair — a student unable to pass an examination, and who wanted to c-copy the answers t-to the paper. And t-then I knew how the sleepers came to sleep —'

'You promised to show us, Professor,' the chairman said.

'And I will, Mr. Chairman. But first I m-must m-make a preparation. For that I must leave you for a little while — if it is permitted?' The chairman nodded: he looked a little puzzled at the request.

The professor sat forward, his hands on his knees below the table. He pushed back his chair, scraping it noisily over the parquet flooring; and he coughed noisily. With a bow to the chairman, he left the room, closing the door quietly behind him.

* * *

Three-quarters of an hour later five Dilettantes, sat up one by one and took notice of their surroundings. Purcell, the mathematician and Charles the psychiatrist were the last to recover, a matter of two minutes after the others. They gaped with astonishment at the table round which they were sitting. In front of each man was a little pile of personal belongings taken from the pockets of the jacket of each of them. Of the professor there was no sign . . .

Until . . .

The door of the service-room opened and a chuckle was followed by the big goblin-like hair shock of Marcus Stubbs. He was still chuckling as he took his chair, and placed his hands on the table.

'It is that I must apologize,' he said. 'But it was necessary to convince you that I knew how the sleep was induced. You feel no more effects than the four people who went to sleep?'

The chairman hesitated. The anger which had shown in his colour subsided slowly, and he grinned a little sheepishly. 'I feel no after-effects, Professor,' he said. 'But it is an experience I shall remember.'

The A.C. was regarding the logician gravely. 'I think you had better explain,' he said. The professor smiled, and danced his fingers on the table.

'Oh, Oh!' he said, gleefully. 'Sir Edward has the idea that I am the sleep-maker. I assure him I do not know Mr. Abrahams, nor Mr Gibbs. Nor the g-glamorous Adèle and the d-diamond man.'

'What did you use?' the A.C. demanded.

'This!' He produced from a pocket a glass globe, about the size of the kind used as Christmas decorations, and placed it on the table. Sir Edward reached out for it. The professor shooed him away. 'We must be very careful,' he said. 'If it breaks we will all go to sleep again. Now, I will tell you how I, Marcus Stubbs, Professor of Logic, solved the mystery of the sleepers.' He fished out his snuff box, and took the usual two pinches, dusting his lapels after the operation. Then he commenced his explanation — addressing the A.C.

'You described t-the examination of t-the c-contents of Gibbs's car, Sir Edward,' he said. 'The dust, the w-white p-powder, and the shivers of very thin glass convex curved, which had come from the wrist-watch of Gibbs. This, I d-did not l-like at all. B-because, you see, when the glass of a watch is broken by violence it does not g-go into slivers; it breaks in tiny rectangular pieces, or strips. Also the c-curvature of a watch glass is so slight that a sliver w-would show little or no convex appearance.

'I said to m-myself if it was n-not from a watch-face — then f-from w-what did it come? Then it w-was that from my dormant mind I r-recalled the s-student in Bonn who by a trick copied out t-the answers to his examination p-paper. And I knew the explanation. Or, I t-thought I did. B-but I must p-prove it.' He fingered the glass ball on the table gently. 'I b-bought four of these from a shop,' he said. 'And then I took them to a friend who has a laboratory and talked to him —'

'Then it was gas?' the A.C. said. The professor nodded.

'T-there is only one gas, so the laboratory at Bonn said many years ago, that, used in small quantities, can emulate 'la natural' illness, s-such as f-faintness and syncope, and leave no ascertainable cause. That is *hydrogen-arsenide*. It c-can also kill if used in sufficient strength, and the death will in all p-probability be p-put down to n-natural death. S-so I s-searched. T-there are few glass blowers in L-London who m-make such t-trifles as these: and I f-found one w-who had had an order for two dozen such with onion-skin thin glass. I w-went to the customer — a shop specializing in decorations and, w-with persuasion p-purchased four. My l-laboratory friend filled them w-with the gas, which he made. I must p-prove to you that I am right. So, one ball I try on myself in my room. And I sleep. Two balls I try on you because this is a large room. And you sleep.' The professor, in his excitement was losing his stammer again. 'The fourth ball is here for Sir Edward.

'The puzzle of the sleepers is answered. Such a ball was tossed through the open window of Abrahams and Hemingway, and when the men were overcome the thrower entered the rooms and robbed. Such a ball was dropped in the car of Miss Narraway and that of Gibbs. The balls, under pressure of the gas break at the slightest knock. The noise is slight: you did not hear it because

I scraped my chair on the floor when I threw them under this table.' He chortled a little. 'But they leave shivers of glass, Sir Edward, and your men missed such shivers in the rooms of the old money-lender and the diamond setter.' The professor sat back. 'That is the mystery — solved,' he said. 'I am forgiven?'

The chairman smiled. 'So far as I am concerned, yes. And I am sure Sir Edward is pleased.'

The A.C. nodded, slowly. 'But it doesn't lead us to the operator,' he said.

The professor, leaned forward. His fingers felt in a waist-coat pocket, and came out with his snuff box. Almost caressingly, he lifted a pinch, and sniffed it. His eyes behind the thick lenses rested on the A.C. and he nodded his goblin-like shock of hair, understandingly.

'It s-should n-not be difficult, Sir Edward,' he said. 'Two dozen such balls were ordered. They are, as I h-have s-said, very frail, and he t-took only six from t-the shop who g-got them for him. He is, you will agree, successful in his v-ventures. He w-will, I have no doubt, go back for more. The shop is Brewsters in Soho.'

30

THE discussion at the gathering of the Dilettantes on Thursday evening, July 23rd, 1959 was desultory: without pattern and with no academic standard. It was the last meeting before the summer recess and the members, jaded by the heat of the warmest summer for years, were regarding with mental anticipation their coming vacation — not from the club: but from the workaday exactment of their various callings. Thus nobody had prepared a paper for debate; and after dinner conversation became a causerie of such insignificant and unscholarly topics as come casually to the mind.

The spark was struck by Norman Charles. The psychiatrist had just moved house into a luxury flat, and was warm in praise of the central heating — warmed floors; he referred to the modern methods of building. Professor Stubbs first snorted, and then giggled.

'Modern!' he ejaculated. '*O sancta simplicitas!* W-what man has f-forgotten, man can remember. Mr. Charles, the Roman Emperor, Caracalla, heated his baths and s-sports building on the Appian Way by the floors in t-the year 217.'

'The deuce he did,' said Charles.

'The floors were warm to the touch from steam passing be-beneath t-them, Mr. Charles.' He paused. 'W-what is t-there in our time that is new? Was it Priestley in the nineteenth century who g-gave us the b-blessings of anaesthetics for surgery, Sir Noël?' He looked across at the chairman. 'Yet Homer in the *Odyssey* tells us of Helen's drug given in wine 'to induce oblivion to all ills', and the physician, Galen, d-did he n-not in the second century practise the use of mandragora to paralyse sensation. Inter-communication so t-that we c-can speak to any r-room in a building — is t-that new? Then how w-was it that Lucretia Borgia could in her boudoir hear everything t-that was s-spoken in any room in her p-palace? The microphone and loud speaker t-that carries a v-voice to all parts of a t-theatre — would t-that be a modern invention? The voices of speakers were sent to every c-corner of the Roman Forum by loud speakers. And shorthand, so necessary to modern b-business; was it n-not used to report Cato's speech on t-the Castilinian Conspiracy in B.C. 63? Pitman and Bright! Phooey! A freed slave in Rome invented shorthand; and man forgot it until, in 1588, Bright resurrected it.'

'Is there *nothing* new under the sun, then, Professor?' James asked; and there was sarcasm in the cadences of his voice.

'Apart f-from electronics and atomics I s-should say no — if sufficient research is made. Nor, g-gentlemen is there anything w-which one man c-can c-conceive in secret t-that another man c-cannot find out and combat. T-there was an antidote to the m-magnetic mine; and Radar defeated the silent rocket.'

Purcell, who is a mathematician, chuckled. 'A writer invents a plot for a detective novel, Professor. If it can be solved by another, then the novel is useless, since the denouement surprise is the only real interest. What about the conception there?'

'I have n-never read a d-detective novel, Mr. Purcell, w-without knowing the identity of the c-criminal while only half-way through, w-when the s-story is properly and fairly told. But t-the r-reading must be thorough, weighing the evidence of each s-sentence, and no reading a line w-with one g-glance of the eyes. Given t-that, and the exercise of logical deduction, no denouement is possible; there is b-but one answer.' He bowed slightly to the Assistant Commissioner. 'Sir Edward knows very well t-that w-what the mind of a malefactor conceives in real crime, the m-minds of his detectives c-can discover.'

'Sometimes, Professor,' the A.C. said. 'But not always.'

'That is b-because you miss vital points, Sir Edward. T-that is all.'

The A.C. smiled. 'I am tempted to test you on that, Professor. There is, for instance, the Chelsea flat puzzle.'

The chairman clapped his hands.

'Excellent,' he said, and became enthusiastic. 'Evidence, Edward — for the Professor.'

* * *

'You have probably read the details given in the newspapers,' the A.C. began. 'There is, however, much that we have not told the Press. I will, therefore, go into the details in full and from the beginning. The beginning is with Mrs. Chloe Hart, a charwoman, who for eighteen months had 'done for' Miss Alicia Menston at the latter's flat in Clawston House, Tite Street, Chelsea. On Tuesday morning — that is three days ago — Mrs. Hart arrived at Clawston House, walked up the hall to the flat, produced her key and opened the flat door, calling out 'good morning, miss,' as she hung up her hat and coat in the lobby. She then opened the door into the lounge — and immediately ran out of the flat, shrieking that Miss Menston had been murdered.

'And she had. The woman was reclining, apparently restfully, on the settee. She was still in the evening frock she had worn the previous night — an elaborate affair in ivory lace over a pink under-slip. She had been strangled with her own silk scarf. According to the police surgeon she had been dead between nine and ten hours, which puts the time of the murder between 11 o'clock and midnight on the previous night. The room was in complete disorder. A couple of chairs were lying on their sides, ornaments had been knocked to the floor and broken, cushions had been flung on the floor. Drawers of an escritoire had been pulled out and their contents scattered around. The same thing had been done in the bedroom adjoining: the woman's clothes from the wardrobe and the contents of the drawers and dressing-table being thrown pell-mell. It was, in fact, complete devastation — except for a large cupboard in the lounge which ran from floor to ceiling, and was some three feet deep with shelves starting breast-high. The lower shelves contained wines and cocktail bottles and glasses; those at the top carried cardboard boxes bearing the names of *couturières* and millinery establishments. This was undisturbed; the contents were obvious at a glance and could have hidden nothing.'

'Any m-marks of violence on t-the b-body apart from the strangling?' the professor asked.

'None whatever.'

31

'Now I will deal with the happenings of the previous night.' The A.C. considered for a moment, with brows furrowed in an effort to remember accurately the details. 'That you may properly appreciate them I shall have to give you the outlay. Clawston House is a block of flats, constructed out of three large houses, modernized. There are three flats on the ground floor, each consisting of a small lobby, a lounge, a bedroom, bathroom, lavatory and kitchen. These three flats are situated at the end of the hall opposite the entrance door. Flat No. 1 is on the left, its door being hidden from view by the staircase and lift to the upper floor. This flat is unoccupied at the moment, the tenant being abroad. The door of Flat No. 2, which was that of the dead woman, is in full view from the hall. The door of Flat No. 3 is invisible from the hall being just inside a passage at right angles leading to a side door — the tradesmen's entrance both to the three ground-floor flats, and those on the upper floor, access to which is gained by stone steps from the end of the passage. This side-door is the only entrance to the building other than the front door. In the hall, opposite the lift and staircase is the porter's desk, his cubby-hole and the telephone switchboard. This commands a full view of the entrance and the length of the hall from the front door to the flats. This fact is important.

'Now for the events of the previous afternoon and night. Miss Menston entered her flat at 5.15 in the afternoon, speaking to the day porter, Leslie Sandall, as she passed him. Sandall says she remained in her flat until 7 o'clock. At 6.45 a man in evening dress and overcoat called on the girl. He was known to both porters as a Mr. Roland Jennings, a man about town, and a friend of Miss Menston. At 7 o'clock he came out with the girl, and they left in a taxi which the porter called for them. The porter passed on the address to the driver — the Mayfair Club. Sandall says there were no callers at the flat up to 10 o'clock when he went off duty and was replaced by the night porter, Alfred Bowes. The only visitor to the building at all was a chauffeur with a letter to Mrs. Heather who occupies Flat 3. He delivered it and, returning down the hall after a couple of minutes left the building.

'Bowes says that Jennings and Miss Menston returned to the flat at 10.30. They went in together; and a few minutes later either turned on the radio or played gramophone records — there was a portable gramophone and a supply of records in the lounge — for he says the music was so loud that he was about to go and protest at the volume when it suddenly stopped. At 11 o'clock the flat door opened and Mr. Jennings appeared. He was talking to the girl, and finally said: 'See you at 3 o'clock to-morrow then, Alicia,' pulled the door to, walked down the hall, said goodnight to the porter and left. In less than a minute he was back. 'It's raining!' he said to the porter. 'Will you ring for a taxi?' The porter did so, and they stood chatting while waiting.'

The A.C. paused, and pointed a finger impressively at the Dilettantes. 'Now, a couple of minutes later they were startled by a shout from Miss Menston's flat. It was a woman's voice, and the shout was followed by the words:

'No, no . . . please.' The two looked at each other and went simultaneously to the flat door. Jennings knocked and called out: 'Is anything wrong, Alicia?' There was a pause and then Miss Menston's voice said: 'Who is it?' Jennings repeated his inquiry and said: 'You were shouting.' A laugh came back and then: 'I'm all right, darling. Shouting? It's on the wireless.' With that the two men went away, and Mr. Jennings left the building. It is important that Jennings and the porter were closely questioned separately on the episode, and their accounts corroborated, with minor differences, each other. Only two other people entered the hall after that, and they were occupants of an upstairs flat, and went up in the lift.

'Now occurs the second odd happening. At 11.20 o'clock a telephone call came for Miss Menston. The porter put the call through to her flat and listened to ensure connection was made. *A man's voice answered and in reply to a call for Miss Menston replied: 'She can't speak to you now. Ring to-morrow!'.'*

'Who was the man?' Charles asked. The A.C. shook his head. 'I'm outlining the story,' he said. 'I'll go into the investigating later. The porter said he was a little non-plussed by a man being in the flat, and was puzzled as to how he had got in without his having seen him; but he said it was not his business who tenants had in their flats at night and he put the matter out of his mind. Nobody else entered the building that night and nobody left; and not until the arrival of the charwoman at 8 o'clock was there any evidence of anything untoward. Those are the vital facts in the case, Professor, and when I have wet my whistle with another glass of the chairman's Port, I will go into more details.'

Five minutes were spent in appreciating the wine, and in choosing and lighting up cigars. Not until the five were comfortably relaxed and settled again did the A.C. resume. 'Well, what do you want to know first, Professor?' he asked. Before Stubbs could reply Purcell broke in. 'The girl, and the motive. Always start with the motive. Golden rule isn't it? Who was the girl?'

'We know little about her, so far,' the A.C. replied. 'She was about 26 years of age and was for sometime a show-girl in the theatre. But for a couple of years she has done no work of any kind. She was well known in the West End, particularly in night club circles, and was usually escorted by well-to-do men. She lived luxuriously, the flat, for instance, is a very expensive-looking nest.'

'A kept woman?' the chairman suggested.

'Not that we have discovered, Noël.'

'Call girl most likely,' said Charles.

'Not in those flats, Charles. It would have been spotted.'

'Then what?'

'Ah, there we come to motive. And that is problematical. She had a number of men friends. Their names were in her diary. All of them have been seen, and all admit that they occasionally gave her presents. Asked what kind of presents they gave a figure; and adding their separate statements into a whole, the girl must have had something like £6,000 over a couple of years from these men alone —'

'And there may be others?' the chairman asked.

'I think it most likely.'

'And she did not, of course, pay for her entertainment and eats, and so on. She was taken out.'

'Yes — and that brings forward another odd fact,' the A.C. said. 'Because she had no money except for a few pounds, no bank account, no safe deposit. On the afternoon of her death one man said he had given her £100 in notes at 4 o'clock. She had £5 when the body was found.'

'Taken by the murderer,' Charles suggested.

'Then why did he leave the £5?'

'Anyhow, there's hardly a motive in 'the men's presents',' James suggested. 'They gave her money in return for favours received, I suppose. If they wanted to quit all they had to do was to end the paying. They didn't have to kill — any of them.'

'If they *could* quit,' the A.C. said. 'There is rather an odd circumstance in connection with that, too. She had a small circle of women friends. One of them, whose name I don't propose to mention, said that a week or so ago when she was referring enviously to Menston's men friends and the presents she must get from them, received the reply: 'That would be fine if I didn't have to give it away. But I'm getting fed up, and don't intend to do so much longer.' A rather significant statement, taken in conjunction with the fact that she has no capital from the £6,000 or more she had received.'

'You mean they couldn't quit because she was blackmailing them. Is that your theory? And she was killed by one of them. But what about the absence of the fruits of blackmail, A.C.?' James asked.

'It is not my theory,' Sir Edward said.

'But the theory of my investigating officers is that she was a blackmailer's stooge and passed on the money to her employer, or bully, who maintained her in the flat, clothes, etc.'

'Oh!' the chairman said. 'And the murderer killed thinking she *herself* was the blackmailer?'

The A.C. nodded. 'A murder which would be without release,' he said. Then: 'Well, Professor, that is all the data we have on the woman and the manner of her death. But there are a few points in the investigation into the actual

crime. I am giving you every chance to prove your asser-
tions, you see.'

The professor grunted. 'W-what are the p-points, Sir
Edward?' he demanded.

'These: We have accounted for every person known to
have entered the building, or left it, between 6 o'clock at
night and 8 o'clock next morning. The hall desk is never
left vacated —'

'Question?' The professor interrupted. 'D-does the
porter not, for instance, make tea, or coffee, or eat a meal?'

'He does — but in his cubby-hole, which still gives him
a complete view of all the hall directly in front of him, the
staircase and lift; to his left the front entrance; to his right
he has only to look out of the corner of his eye to see the
flats. He cannot leave because of the telephone switchboard, which he works.' The A.C. paused, waiting. There
was no response from the professor; and he continued,
enumerating the points on his fingers: 'At 5.15 Miss
Menston returned to her flat. At 9.25 the visitor — a chauffeur — called with a letter and delivered it to Mrs. Heath
in Flat No. 3 —'

'Why did not the porter deliver it?' the professor asked.
'He s-seems to have delivered the p-post.'

'Because the man said he was to deliver it personally.
Anyway he went to the flat door round the corner of the
side passage. He was out of sight for less than two minutes
and then left as he had entered, by the hall front entrance.
At 6.45 Jennings came; at 7 o'clock he and the girl left.
Nobody went near the flat from then until 10.30 when
Jennings and the girl returned. At 11 o'clock Jennings came
out. Nobody was seen to go into or come out of her flat
after that until the charwoman found the girl murdered.

'*Now, Professor, who killed Miss Menston? Who got in
that flat after 11 o'clock when Jennings left, when the girl*

was still alive; and murdered her and wrecked the room. And answered a telephone call at 11.20? Remember there is no way in or out of that buildings except the front door, and past the porters.'

'There is, you know, Edward,' the chairman said. 'The side door at the end of the cross passage, the tradesmen's entrance. He could get in and out through that.'

The A.C. grinned. 'I thought you had all overlooked that, Noël.' He shook his head, sadly. 'But it doesn't help you. The door is closed and fastened from the inside at 6 o'clock in the evening. There had been several intruders in the past, and that was the strict rule. It was so closed that night; and it was still closed after the discovery of the murder.'

'Locked?'

'No. Closed from inside by a thumbscrew bolt — you know the kind of thing: a long oval knob which you turn with your fingers, and which then shoots a steel bolt into a hole in the lintel. The only known safe way of avoiding burglarious entry by a door.'

'One more question, Edward,' the chairman said. 'The man Jennings, was he being blackmailed?'

'He denies it emphatically. He says he never gave her anything except a good time in the West End, and then never more than once a month, as he couldn't afford it. The time limit is corroborated by inquiries.'

'Would he have been the bully to whom she gave the presumed blackmail money?' Charles asked.

'If he was he is remarkably lacking in the proceeds, Charles. His bank account seems to linger around a regular £300.'

'Then it is up to the Professor,' the chairman said. 'We had better give him a few minutes to gather the fragments of his arguments.'

He rang the bell, and ordered coffee.

32

THE professor sat back in his chair, with his head forward, hiding his gig-lamp spectacles and the eyes behind them. His coffee-cup rested, untouched on the table in front of him. Thus he stayed for some minutes while his fellow Dilettantes jested with each other, and the A.C. Then, suddenly, he sat up, threw back his head and laughed. They watched him, exasperation in their looks. He apologized, and drew the old silver snuff box from a waistcoat pocket and took two pinches from it. Very deliberately he replaced it, and dusted his lapels with a handkerchief. Then he spoke — three words which electrified the waiting company.

'The bungling fool!' he said.

It sounded as though he regarded the bungling as a personal affront. And it seemed that he spoke almost to himself, for at an exclamation from Charles he looked up and became apparently aware of the waiting Dilettantes; and his comment.

'Yes, a bungling fool,' he said again. Look at t-the *Mise-en-scène*. There are overturned c-chairs and b-broken ornaments to suggest violence. B-but there is n-no evidence of violence on t-the w-woman apart from strangulation. It w-would seem from her position t-that she was resting on the settee. Then w-why, gentlemen, the overturned furniture, the s-smashed ornaments. And w-why the scattered clothes, and papers, the outflung c-cushions — the scene of devastation, as Sir Edward has called it?

'I w-will tell you — I, Marcus Stubbs, the logician. This bungler has r-read too many d-detective stories and w-watched too much t-television crime. My friends, every w-work of art has what experts call *class* — spontaneity and love of the work. But few of t-them are p-perfect.

There is bad drawing in Goya, and there are d-dispropor-
tions in Velasquez. But a copyist, an imitator, never puts
them into his copy. He is not spontaneous; he is t-too
intent on painting the detail correctly. He works with a
self-consciousness and meticulous care which the c-cre-
ative artist never exhibits. So you c-can always pick out
the c-copy however excellent it may be p-painted. It is
so in t-this c-case. Look, I ask you again, at the *mise-en-
scène* — the emptied drawers, the scattered clothes. T-they
are the hallmarks of television crime and the d-detective
novel. On television it is necessary to exaggerate. But t-tell
me, Sir Edward' — he turned and demanded the attention
of the A.C. — 'have you, or your policemen ever k-known
before any searcher after something c-create such havoc?'

Sir Edward Allen shook his head. 'I confess — it is a
little unusual,' he said.

'What *d-do* you find?'

'Usually drawers left partly open with their contents
muddled up. Sometimes a few articles spilled on the floor.
Possibly in wardrobes dresses or suits fallen to the floor —
and so on.'

'B-but never c-clothes scattered all over rooms. No. So
we h-have a d-drama staged down to t-the last d-detail
like a Zola novel —'

'You mean, Stubbs — ?'

'That t-there w-was no search for anything. Sir
Edward; only a *mise-en-scène* to suggest a searching. The
murderer w-was safe in the flat, secure from interruption
until day-light. Why t-the haste t-to find something?' He
paused to sample once again his snuff box and to drain his
coffee now cold; with his eyes still on the face of the A.C.
watching him. He set the cup back in the exact centre of
the saucer. 'So we d-dispose of the m-murderer's search
for, shall we say a non-existent instrument of b-black-

mail. Except, t-that is, for t-the cupboard, which w-was strangely undisturbed. Tell me, Sir Edward, w-was there a key to the c-cupboard?'

'There was one found on the floor, yes. It had apparently fallen from the key hole.'

'So!' The professor nodded his head as though in confirmation of something that had come into his mind when he asked the question. 'We will now leave the flat' (he went on) 'and return to t-the hall. *Hélas!* It is 6 o'clock. Miss Menston has returned and gone into her flat. She is still there. Sandall leaves his desk and switchboard and walks towards the flats. He turns into the passage, past the door of Flat No. 3, and at t-the end of it, he turns t-the b-bolt at the side door. There is n-now no way into the flats except b-by way of the f-front door, and the porter. *Nobody* passes the porter to approach the f-flats until 9.25 w-when a m-man in uniform arrives with a letter in his hand for Flat No. 3, which he must deliver personally. He goes round the corner of the side passage, and returns within a c-couple of minutes without the letter. W-what w-was the nature of the m-message to Mrs. Heather, Sir Edward?'

The A.C. stared. 'I don't know, Professor,' he said. 'So far as I know it was not inquired into. Why should it be? The man remained on the premises only two or three minutes, and Miss Menstone was alive at 11 o'clock, an hour and three quarters after this man had gone. I fail to see any connection.'

The professor waved his hands. He shook his goblin-like shock of hair. 'But it is of t-the utmost importance,' he insisted. 'Of all t-the p-people who c-came into this sealed enclosure only he is unknown.' He leaned forward earnestly, spread his hands on the table, and spoke: *'I d-do n-not think Mrs. Heather had any letter or v-visitor that night. If she d-did, then t-there is no sense or reason in t-the conditions in that flat.'*

The A.C. drummed with his fingers on the table, and hesitated a few moments. Then lifting the telephone on a wall stand he asked for Scotland Yard, and spoke to the inspector on duty. 'This Menston business, Rowntree,' he said. 'Do you know who was the man who called on Flat No. 3 that night? . . .Yes, that's right, the man in uniform. You don't? . . . No, of course I understand that. Look here, telephone Mrs. Heather and ask her his name and business, and by whom he is employed. Telephone me back to this number, Les. 0212.' He replaced the receiver. 'Yes, Professor?' he invited.

'So we come to 10.30 and the return of Jennings and the woman,' the professor continued with his recital. 'What c-can I, a Professor of Logic, make of the s-strange h-happenings from then until 11.20? There is a n-noisy p-playing of music, and then silence. There is t-the exit of Jennings with his p-parting words: 'See you at 3 o'clock'. Was that a little odd, do you t-think?'

'In what way odd?' Purcell asked.

'Has he n-not told the p-police that his association w-with the girl was taking her out in the West End once a m-month. And a check on t-this, Sir Edward says, c-confirmed the period. W-why then is he doubling the entertainment, on this night of all n-nights? But w-we will pass it for the moment.'

33

THE buzzing of the telephone had interrupted the professor. Sir Edward crossed to the instrument, lifted the receiver, and listened for no longer than a minute.

Replacing it with studied carefulness he returned to his chair and turned to the odd little man, who was waiting to continue.

'That was Inspector Rowntree,' he said. 'Mrs. Heather says she had no caller or letter that night.'

'Ah! It is b-beginning to fall into place,' the professor said, and shook his mop of hair. 'Where w-were we? Oh, yes. Jennings had c-come out of the flat and closed the door. He walked p-past the p-porter and out of the hall. And a minute later he is b-back again, and then t-they hear the woman call out —'

'He came back because it was raining, Professor,' the chairman said. 'He wanted a taxi.'

The professor nodded. 'He would h-have come back in any case, Sir Noël. He *had* to come back. It w-was essential that he s-should be in that hall for at least five minutes after he l-left the flat. It must be s-shown that t-the woman was alive then.'

The A.C. looked up sharply at this statement, and laughed. 'I appreciate the point you are about to make,' he said. 'It *had* occurred to us. We disproved it.'

The professor eyed him, and there was a challenge in the glance. 'I wonder,' he said. 'We w-will come b-back to it later. Meantime, consider the w-woman Menston. She w-was a showgirl but had done no work for t-two years. And all the t-time she is l-living well with an escort of well-off men.' He paused. 'I h-have no doubt the detective officers are right, that she w-was an instrument of blackmail and t-that she passed on the money to her employer —'

'And a victim killed her,' James said. 'But how, Professor, in that closed room which could not be entered or left without the porter seeing?'

'You jump to c-conclusions, Mr. James. I do n-not think wealthy young Mayfair men would kill to end b-blackmail.

And certainly n-not in so planned a way as this. Killing is t-too dangerous if one c-can afford to pay a regular sum for, shall we say, p-protection. No, let us l-look more c-closely at Miss Menston. She is the envy of her girl friends w-with a collection of men of means in whose c-company she is seen. One of the friends says so. And how significant is the r-reply she re-receives: 'It would be fine if I didn't have to give it (the money) away. B-but I don't intend to do it much longer.' W-what did she mean by that, gentlemen?' The professor chuckled. 'Do y-you s-suppose contrition and the pangs of conscience had w-worked on her — a w-woman of that kind? Or do you t-think that she was herself turning to menaces to h-have more money sticking to her f-fingers? And her instrument? More m-money, or I give you away to the p-police. Either she sends w-word by his messenger — he w-would not be likely to have d-direct contact with her — or he himself gets to hear of the conversation. So she has *t-to be silenced*: thus we g-get to the flat in Clawston House and the b-bungling mess made of the c-contents – all except the wine cupboard.' He turned to the A.C. 'Why do you s-suppose t-that was not ravished like the other p-places, Sir Edward?'

The A.C. shrugged his shoulders. 'I can't say, Professor. Perhaps it was locked.'

'But, w-was the key not on the floor?'

The chairman interposed. 'Professor, you are angling to be asked why the cupboard was not disordered.' The professor chuckled delightedly at the riposte. 'It is an old trick of yours. But we will play with you. Why was it not disordered?'

The professor chuckled again. He was enjoying the duel. And he had the interests of the Dilettantes so closely that their cigars had gone out and their glasses held untasted port. Once again he produced his snuff box and took the two habitual pinches, bending over the table as he did so. Then he blew a few grains of dust from the table top, looked up and continued.

'I w-wonder, ah, I wonder.' He spoke as though to himself his eyes staring in front, past the men watching him. *'Did he see the m-murder committed, or d-did he just c-close his eyes and pray?'*

Shock held the Dilettantes silent for a moment or two. It sent them rigid in their chairs. The chairman's hand going up to his mouth with a lighted match for his cigar halted, as it were, in mid air. Sir Edward Allen was a full ten seconds before he found his voice.

'Saw the murder committed?' he asked. 'Of whom are you speaking?'

'Of the man hiding in the c-cupboard, of course. Of whom else?' He conjured up a look of blank surprise that the question needed to be put.

'What man?' The A.C. spoke sharply.

'The man in the chauffeur's uniform who went with a letter he never delivered to Flat No. 3.'

The A.C. protested. 'He left the building within two minutes. The porter saw him come and go. That was at 9.25, an hour before the girl and Jennings returned to the flat.'

'Tell me. Sir Edward, t-then, who w-was the man who answered the t-telephone at 11.20 and said that Miss Menston w-was not available? No other man w-was known to have entered the Clawston House block at any time.'

'Then he killed her,' Purcell said. 'Nobody else was there.' Purcell waited a moment. 'Isn't that so, Professor?'

'It is true t-that there was n-nobody other than he and the g-girl in the room after 11 o'clock,' the professor said. 'But —' He shrugged his shoulders. 'Now I will tell you, Sir Edward, of the things that h-happened in that flat that night — t-the things t-that *must* have happened, because there is no o-other logical explanation.

'It is of a macabre such as Poe c-could engender in his mind. But t-there is, too, grim comedy. It begins at 9.25, when the supposed chauffeur arrived with a letter for Flat No. 3. He w-was not unknown to the flats, but a uniform and a peaked c-cap is an excellent disguise. He knew the habits of the flats and he k-knew Miss Menston, for he h-had a key to her door. Now, w-why did he come. He d-did not deliver any letter to No. 3. Yet t-there must have been some p-purpose for the visit. And the visit had to be concluded in the side passage. T-there is but one logical reason for that.

'*He wanted to unbolt that side door.* But he m-must be seen to leave the building; t-that was essential for his safety. And he *is* so seen. Then, some t-time later — it is impossible to s-say w-what time — he comes again to the flats, through the side door, and he waits for the attention of the p-porter to be diverted, p-perhaps by a telephone call on the s-switchboard, and slips the two or three feet to the door of Miss Menston's flat. He is s-searching for s-something, p-perhaps a letter, for he is one of the v-victims of blackmail.

'What a night, and a t-time to choose. For almost at once he hears a k-key being inserted in the front door, and he hears voices. W-where to hide? The bedroom? If it is a man w-with the girl this girl — he c-can be sure they will g-go into the b-bedroom. There is only the big cupboard. Into it he g-goes, and to make sure he will not be discovered he l-locks the door *from inside* —'

'Since he had to leave the flats by the way you say he came in, if he is not to be seen, how comes it that the door was found still bolted next morning, Professor?' the chairman asked.

'Faugh! Any schoolboy c-could do that, Sir Noël. There are a dozen ways. The most simple? Slip a pair of tweezers along the thumb-screw knob, and have fastened to them a length of twine which is passed underneath the door. Go out, close the door, pull gently but steadily on the twine and the t-tweezers will turn the knob and bolt the door. A sharp tug, and the t-tweezers come away from the knob, and are drawn under the door.

'B-but we m-must go back to the man in the c-cupboard. We k-know who comes in the r-room — Miss Menston and the man Jennings. Presently someone — I s-should say Jennings — turns on the radio or a gramophone. I w-wonder whether the girl suggested a drink, and wondered why the door was fastened, and what the charwoman had done with the key. Can you imagine t-the man inside, terrified and cowering as she tried the door?

'But w-worse was to come. Do you t-think he p-peered through the keyhole to see who w-was the man with the g-girl? And if he did, what d-did he see?'

The professor ceased speaking; he looked at the faces of the men sitting round the table.

'What did he see?' he asked again.

Nobody answered him. They sat still and tense, the aura of drama over them. The professor waited. He took out his snuff box, and sniffed from between finger and thumb; and he did not bother this time to dust the fragments from his jacket. Then he spoke:

'I, Marcus Stubbs, will tell your policemen, Sir Edward, w-what he saw t-through the k-keyhole. He saw the girl Menston sitting relaxed on the settee. He s-saw the man Jennings approach her from b-behind bend over and s-slip a scarf under her chin, pull it t-tight round her neck and k-knot it. For, you see, if Alicia Menston were to talk, Othello's occupation would be g-gone.

'He saw Jennings s-stage the search w-with a scatter-ing of belongings, overturn the c-chairs and so on. And, in his terror, but doubtless unable n-not to l-look, he saw Jennings put on his hat and coat, and from the c-coat pocket take a disc and place it on the gramophone, which he wound up. And he saw him leave the flat, speaking f-from the d-door as if to someone inside.

'And, suddenly, when he is about to c-come out of the c-cupboard he is terrified once again by a shout c-coming from the room, and a knocking on the door, and a voice from inside saying 'I'm all right.' Then, when everything has calmed down, he slips out of the flat into the passage and through the side door, bolting it as I h-have explained, b-behind him.'

The professor sat back, his hands spread on the table in front of him. He looked at the A.C. 'I w-win my c-chal-lenge,' he said confidently.

The A.C. cleared his throat. 'In the matter of the gram-ophone —' he began, and was interrupted at once.

'Ah, yes, Sir Edward,' the professor said. 'You s-said t-that you had seen what I was about to s-say, and had disproved it. But, my friend, because a label on a gramo-phone disc bears a famous name, and says it is a Beethoven Symphony or some of the Etudes of Chopin, it d-does not f-follow that the music is that same.

'Play all the records over, Sir Edward — *before Mr. Jennings in his solicitude to take care of Miss Menston's possessions can take one away.*'

34

THE last of the Dilettantes' dinners for October, 1959 — the actual date was Thursday, the 22nd — was rendered distinctive by three circumstances. The first was that, for the first time in its history, the club was invaded by a guest; the second: that its dinner was an invitation occasion, the Assistant Commissioner (Sir Edward Allen) having asked for the privilege of being host to the club, a request which had been granted with acclamation. The third of the distinctive circumstances is a matter for explanation, later, if explanation should, in fact, be necessary.

It was due to Sir Edward's position as host that the guest was introduced. Detective-Inspector Kenway had figured in all the cases which the A.C. had brought to the attention of the Dilettantes; Sir Edward had suggested that the club men might be interested in meeting personally the inspector as distinct from meeting him only in repute: the more so as he would figure in the strange story with which he (the A.C.) would regale the club after dinner.

Sir Edward's reputation as a *gourmet* was well-known to the Dilettantes and the menu with which he had confronted Signor Moroni justified his reputation. With the rich lobster soup — *Bisque de Homard* — went Misa's Abolengo, a fine dry Amontillado; the *Escalopes de Turbot au Champagnes* were eaten to Clos Arlot Blanc, one of the *Prémièries Cuvées* of the Commune of Prémeaux. This was followed by *Selle de pré aux Laitues Braisées* with, to accompany it, Château Langoa-Barton, a fine claret of the Troisièmes Crus classes de medoc. Finally, the *Chartreuse de Perdreaux* was hailed as a supreme achievement of gastronomic excellence on the part of Moroni. The young partridge meat had been removed from the bone and put in a charlotte mould which had been lined with cabbage. To go with it the A.C. had chosen as the wine a Clos de la Calannière. The sweet was Bombe Francillon, an ice-cream made in a mould lined with coffee ice-cream with brandy inside.

It was 9 o'clock before the culinary delight came to an end, and the tottery waiter removed the club silver from the table, replacing it with a box of cigars, decanters of Port (again the 1927 vintage, which is almost as rare as gold these days) and bowls of nuts; and, closing the doors, left the Dilettantes to themselves — and their guest.

The chairman, Sir Noël Maurice, voiced the feelings of the members in a few words: 'Quite the best dinner I ever remember eating in any part of the world, gentlemen,' he said. There were murmurs of approval. 'If the remainder of the evening lives up to it, it should be the most successful in the club's history.'

'I will do my best,' the A.C. replied. But he said it with less than his usual *bonhomie* or so it seemed to Sir Noël, eyeing him unobtrusively, and with a little puzzlement in his face. The A.C. appeared, he thought, a little embarrassed, distrait. But he put it down to the natural embarrassment of most men when praised to their face by their fellows.

Norman Charles began the evening discussion. 'There is one thing I would like to ask our guest — with your permission, Chairman. He would, I feel, be better able to answer it than the A.C., being an investigating officer. It is a question which interests me as a psychiatrist, and probably the professor as a psychologist.'

Inspector Kenway leaned forward, interested.

'It is this: We have cognisance of, and doubtless have ourselves at some time used the cliché 'Honour among thieves.' What I want to ask is whether this is, indeed, a truism? Is there a code among the criminal classes which binds them in honour not to divulge to the Law information they may possess against another of their kindred, and thus obstruct the course of justice?' He finished and sat back expectantly.

Inspector Kenway smiled; and the smile lit up the thin, aquiline face of the tall, slim figure. Amusement was registered in it. "Grass' is the term, Mr. Charles,' he replied. 'And sometimes 'nark' and 'nose'.' He laughed. 'I assure you nothing could be further from the truth. There is no honour among criminals. The average crook would sell his own mother if, thereby, he could save his own skin. Evidence, you may ask. Scotland Yard has a corps known as the Shadow Squad or Under-Cover Men. Their usefulness depends almost entirely on their acquiring inside information from 'narks,' 'grassers' and other informers. It is true that, occasionally, we do find men who refuse to give information — 'I'm no nark, copper' — then we know that they are themselves involved in the matter under inquiry, and for them to 'nark' would land themselves in the cart for complicity. Oh, no, I assure you, gentlemen, there is no honour among thieves.'

'Suppose, Inspector, there is a big robbery, say £50,000 in bank-notes, and one of the operators is discovered, tried and sentenced. Would he accept the view; 'I'm not taking the rap alone; if I go inside, I'll have company?' Mr. James asked.

Inspector Kenway nodded appreciation of the point. 'Suppose, then, there were four men engaged. And the split is £12,000 each after expenses. If he is certain that his £12,000 is put away for him in a safe place then it is likely that he would keep mum, rather than give the names of his partners and risk all the loot being recovered, in which case Mother Hubbard's cupboard would be bare.' The inspector giggled. 'But my experience is that when he comes out of a 'handful,' which is five years, he would find the money gone. A large proportion of stabbing and coshing attacks in the Metropolitan area are due to purloining of the loot.'

'So there is another axiom gone,' the chairman said. He looked across at the Assistant Commissioner. 'The evening is yours, Edward,' he invited.

Sir Edward Allen flicked a length of ash from his cigar, and looked round at the Dilettantes. He let the monocle fall from a perfectly good left eye to the full length of its silk cord, and began:

'The problem I have brought to-night is an odd affair which may be of particular interest to you, James.' He nodded at the pathologist. 'It presented us with a conflict of evidence from two perfectly honourable people, each convinced of his opinion. *Yet, it was obvious that one of them was completely mistaken. The point was — which one?'*

35

'IT BEGINS with a character named Marcus Silver, who lived in Notting Hill Gate. Silver was a curious character indeed. He walked the back streets of Notting Hill looking, as those who saw him said, like a black bird of prey: for he wore always reaching down to his heels a voluminous cloak that had been black ages ago but which had, because of its age, acquired a rusty tint; a big wide-brimmed hat hiding all his face except the mouth and chin; and rubber-soled shoes that made no sound other than a shuffling.

'Like a bird of prey, I said; those who had business with him knew him indeed for a bird of prey; for Marcus Silver was a usurer and nobody who had borrowed money from him had ever been known to get free of the debt. His money-lending was a legitimate business, legally I mean; but we were pretty sure that he had other interests; there was little doubt in our minds that he was a pretty substantial 'fence' of stolen property, we think of stolen bank-notes, securities and such-like financial loot the realization of which is a matter of great difficulty to anyone not cognisant with financial contacts. But we were never able to lay hands on him, though once he had a narrow escape — a matter of a couple of minutes. That is by-the-bye; I have explained it so that you may have a picture of the man.'

Mr. James interrupted. 'Did he have an account at the Bayswater branch of the Southern Provinces Bank, A.C.?' he asked.

Sir Edward nodded. 'Why?' he asked, in surprise.

'I thought I identified him. I have an account there, and I've seen him on a couple of occasions paying in wads of notes. I thought at the time he looked an ominous personage.'

'Quite. Your bank comes into the story at this stage, James. On a dull afternoon in the last week of September — that is a little more than a fortnight ago — Silver left his house, which is also his office, flapped a way in his long cloak to the Bayswater Branch. In exchange for his cheque he took £500 in one-pound notes. The money was paid over by a cashier who called him 'sir' and was very courteous —'

The chairman looked up. 'Any reason, Edward, for emphasizing that?' he asked. 'Most bank tellers would do the same.'

'Yes, there is a reason. We discovered that the cashier was still owing £20 on a £15 loan. He was the one man we knew who knew where Silver lived because he used to visit the house to pay his instalments on the loan. And he also knew that Silver had £500 and that the numbers of the notes had not been recorded, not being in straight series. The significance of this will be apparent later.

'Well, having obtained the £500, Silver shuffled his way back to Notting Hill Gate looking 'sinisterly like the poster of the Spaniard advertising a brand of port wine' as a constable on street beat described him. The officer saw him enter the house at 3.20 o'clock. We tracked his movements — he was, as you realize, a conspicuous figure impossible to pass without being noticed — and so far as we have been able to discover nobody was in his company, or spoke to him, during the journey either way. The next we knew of Silver was that he was dead.'

The A.C. stopped speaking. He poured out a glass of port, took two or three sips from it, rolled them round his mouth for a moment to taste the bouquet; and selected another Havana from the cigar box which he lighted and pulled into a glow.

'Killed?' The question came from Purcell.

'He had been stabbed twice through the back with a long knife tapered to a point. The police surgeon suggested a cook's knife.'

'It was not left in the body, then?' Charles asked.

'No, and we have not been able to find it. The discovery of the body was made when a postman unable to deliver registered letters, made inquiries of the neighbours. The result was that a constable forced an entrance and found the old man lying on the floor of the room he used as an office. Now, mark several points: the place had not been forcibly entered. Not that that means much because any ordinary mortice-lock key would open the doors of a hundred houses of that kind. They are old houses built about sixty years ago, very cheaply and all of one pattern. There were no signs of disturbance except to the safe which was open, Silver's keys dangling from the lock. There was no £500 in the safe.'

'Any prints on the keys?' asked James.

'None at all. Whoever it was seems to have worn gloves.'

'No clues at all?' Charles put the question.

'I will deal with that. Detective-Inspector Edwins was next on the rota when Scotland Yard was informed. After the place had been finger-printed, etc., Edwins went through the contents of Silver's desk. He found a notebook with various names and telephone numbers. He also found a letter which seems to explain the withdrawal of the £50 from the bank.' The A.C. produced a paper from a pocket. 'This is a copy of the letter,' he said, and read it out:

'Dear sir,

I am anxious to borrow £500 without any intim-ate inquiries. Your name has been given to me as one who could accommodate me with a short-term loan. I have ample security which I will bring with me and leave with you at 7.30 to-morrow night. As I need the money urgently would you please be prepared to pay out at that hour should my secur-ities be satisfactory to you.

K. London.'

'There is one odd feature about the letter, apart from the unusual way of asking for a loan — and that is the fact that it bears no address.'

'Did Mr. London go round for his £500?' Charles asked.

The A.C. shrugged. 'Your guess is as good as mine, Charles. We don't know whether he did or not. Silver had no clerk or other person on the premises.'

'What about the names in the book?' the chairman inquired.

'Clients, I suppose?' James put in.

'Some of them. Others were acquaintances. We checked, of course, and all were accounted for. Only one is really concerned in the case — a Mr. Herman Eisdale.

'Now the Divisional Surgeon who conducted the post-mortem found that both stabs had penetrated the heart from different angles. Death, he said, was instantaneous, and had taken place about 7.30 on the previous night. Technically, his report said at some time between 7 o'clock and 8.30, but if he were asked to give an approximate time then 7.30.

'This, then, seemed to be plain sailing and we started investigations on those lines. Edwins mobilized his men in a search for anyone who might have seen Silver between 3.30 when the constable saw him enter his house, and 7.30 when he died. This brought no results at first but in the evening a Constable Jenkins turned up with a train conductor of the Central London Tube who, he said, had some information. Provided with a comfortable chair in the inspector's office, and a cigarette the man, a Roland Adams, said he certainly had seen Silver that night. Asked where, he replied: 'Midway between Queens Road and Notting Hill Gate Tube stations.' Inspector Edwins asked him if he could fix a time and he replied: 'Sure, chum, half past ten o'clock'.'

'What!' The exclamation came from the pathologist.

'Quite, James!' the A.C. retorted. 'Inspector Edwins was dumbfounded — and showed it. But Adams repeated his statement, and emphatically. To a suggestion that he might be mistaken in the man he replied: 'Nark it, chum, I've known the funny old geezer for years. He lived near me. O' course I seen him.' He explained that his spell of duty ended at Liverpool Street at something after 9.15 and he then took train as passenger to Queen's Road where he was intending to have a drink in a pub until closing time at 10.30. The first person he saw on coming out of the hostelry was 'the old black crow hisself'.'

'Perhaps he got the wrong day,' Purcell suggested.

'The inspector realized the possibility,' the A.C. said. 'Adams's reply was to ask the inspector which night there had been a bit of a disturbance in the road leading to the Russian Embassy at the corner of Kensington Gardens because he had walked into the row after seeing Silver. The inspector agreed that the disturbance had occurred between 10.30 and 10.45 on the night that Silver was killed. Adams then added, as an after-thought that he had called out 'Goodnight' to Silver who had grunted something in reply.'

A knock at the door was followed by the entrance of the aged waiter with a tray containing a silver coffee jug and milk jug, cups and saucers. He placed it on the table — and vanished. The chairman poured out.

'A bit of a p-problem for you, Sir Edward,' the professor said between sips.

36

'IT WAS to become still more involved, Professor,' the A.C. retorted. He drew on his cigar and watched it until the ash was burning evenly again. Then he went on: 'I mentioned that we checked on the people named in the notebook found in Silver's desk. One of the names, as I have said, was Herman Eisdale.' The A.C. paused again and twisted his cigar in his hands. His face was enigmatic. 'We knew something of Eisdale. He owned, or was reputed to own a night-club in Soho — the Two Owls, probably an appropriate name because the club does not open until 11 o'clock at night. It serves meals, and, of course, drink and has a cabaret show at midnight and 2 o'clock in the morning. We think it has other interests including roulette and baccarat. But this we have never been able to prove.'

'W-why do y-you think so?' the professor asked.

'Because men we know to be professional gamblers go in there — and disappear. They are not in the club rooms when our officers enter to see what they are up to. It is also the venue of undesirables of another kind. They are, of course, free to go into a club if they like, providing the club will have them —'

'And m-may n-not know of their c-character,' the professor said.

'Quite so. Mr. Eisdale lives in Hanger Hill, Ealing and Inspector Edwins and a sergeant went to see him. He is a man somewhere about 65 years of age, below normal height with sparse grey hair, obviously well educated but with a slight guttural accent. Told of Silver's death he appeared staggered and asked from what he had died, since he had no idea the man had been ill. The inspector said Silver had been stabbed; upon which Eisdale sank heavily into a chair and said: 'Ghastly. Who'd do a thing like that?' and added: 'poor old Silver.' Then he asked: 'When did this happen, Inspector?'; and was told at 7.30 the previous night.

'At this Eisdale sat up and stared. 'There's something wrong about that, Inspector,' he said. 'I don't say he isn't dead but he certainly wasn't murdered at 7.30 because *he was with me in this flat from 8 until 10 o'clock.*'

It was Edwins' turn to stare. And he did! 'Are you quite sure of that, sir?' he asked. 'Sure? Of course I'm sure,' Eisdale replied. Then a thought occurred to him. 'But how did you know I knew him?' he asked. Edwins produced the notebook with his name and address in. 'I suppose you would be a client?' he suggested. Eisdale laughed. 'Oh, dear no. Nothing like that,' he said. 'We were, I suppose, kind of partners.' Asked to elaborate his answer Eisdale said he had a clientèle in the club who were frequently in temporary financial embarrassment but had handsome expectations. He intimated to such that he knew of a reliable man with a close mouth who would oblige with a loan — and passed them over to Silver, drawing, he said, a commission on the transaction.

'Inspector Edwins tumbled to the fact that the debts could hardly be for food and wines and were most likely from gambling we suspected took place. But he said nothing, other than: 'and getting from the loan the money owed you, I take it?' Eisdale replied: 'Of course. That is business.' 'Why did Silver visit you last night?' the inspector asked. 'On the very night he was murdered.'

"We usually met here once a month to settle my commission and to discuss things' Eisdale replied. 'He had an interest in the club. Last night was the usual monthly call.'

'Now, at this point Edwins asked if Mr. K. London was a member of the club, and one whom he had passed on to Silver. Eisdale wrinkled his brows in thought, and said he couldn't recall the name. Who was Mr. London? Edwins handed him the letter found in Silver's desk. He read it through and handed it back. 'No,' he said. 'I don't know the name, and the writing certainly isn't like any on I.O.U.'s I hold, if that is on your mind. Anyway the johnny certainly couldn't have killed him at 7.30 since Silver was with me more than two hours later.'

"No, I suppose not,' Edwins said.' The A.C. halted and felt in his pockets again. 'It is a little difficult to relate in third person the remainder of the interview,' he said. 'So I propose to read you verbatim notes taken by the sergeant:

'Inspector: Were you alone in the flat?

Eisdale: Yes.

Inspector: Did he have a meal with you here?

Eisdale: Oh, no. I always eat at the club.

Inspector: Anybody else here see Silver?

Eisdale: I couldn't say. The porter may have seen him come.

Inspector: And you wouldn't know whether he had any enemies, I suppose?

Eisdale: I should say he had plenty, Inspector. He was pretty hot on his per cent for loans. I wouldn't have touched him for instance, however badly I needed money.

Inspector: But you passed your members on to him!

Eisdale: That was up to them. If they didn't like his terms when they heard them, they needn't borrow. Were I you, I would look locally for the killer. Friday was his normal day for repayments and he'd have a lot of money in the place. I reckon most of his customers would know that. And I would look round about 10.30. It would have taken him that long to get from here to his house.

Inspector: And you would be where at 10.30?

Eisdale: In the club. We open at 11. You know that, of course.

Inspector: And from 7 to 8 o'clock?

Eisdale: In this flat. Alone, I'm afraid. But I did go down to the porter just before eight for some cigarettes if that's any good to you.'

The A.C. returned the document to his pocket. 'That is the sum total of what Eisdale could tell us,' he said. 'Inspector Edwins left, and in the hall questioned the porter. He agreed that Mr. Eisdale had come down for some cigarettes. That was about 8 o'clock. Then the inspector put another question: 'Do you know a Mr. Silver?'

"What, the old black crow?' the porter said; and added 'that's what we call him here.' Asked when he had last seen

him, he said: 'last night. He came to see Mr. Eisdale just
turned eight o'clock. Nearly frightened me out of me ruddy
wits when I turns round and sees him at me side in that big
hat and his long cloak. I hadn't heard him come in.' Asked
whether by any chance he saw him leave he replied that as
it happened he had: and explained: 'I was just going out
for a coffee and rum on the quiet when I hears Mr. Eisdale
on the first floor landing sing out: 'Good night old boy, it's
a bit late, you'd better let the porter call you a taxi.' So I
waits and the old 'un comes down the stairs. But he said
he didn't want a taxi and I watched him shuffle off along
the street.'

'That would be — what time?' the inspector asked; and
received the reply: 'About five to ten. The café across the
street closes at 10 o'clock, and I just made it.'

'There isn't much more to tell before I pass over the
discussion to you,' the A.C. said. 'Edwins reported back
to me and I, naturally, took the surgeon to task. It was
impossible to accept as dead at 7.30 a man who was seen
alive at 10 o'clock, and again at 10.30.'

'And what did he say to that?' asked James the pathologist.

The A.C. grinned broadly. 'He said he didn't care a damn
what anybody said. The man was dead before 8 o'clock.
That is as far as we have progressed with actual evidence.'

37

SIR Edward relaxed in his chair. He poured out a glass of
Port and slipping his monocle back into his perfectly good
left eye surveyed his fellow Dilettantes. 'I shall be interested to hear how you argue out of that impasse,' he said:
'especially the professor.'

'Firstly, there is one point I would like cleared up,' Charles said. 'You did not mention whether there were any signs of violence on the body, apart from the stabbing?'

'None at all.'

'I see. No forcing of the doors and there was no violence. The inference is either: (1) Silver himself let the attacker into the house; or (2) the attacker had a right of entry and was so well-known to Silver that he had no fear of him.'

'Go on,' the A.C. invited.

'Silver was expecting a visitor at 7.30 to collect £500 on loan. The surgeon says he died at 7.30 and the £500 is gone from the safe.'

'It's too easy,' Purcell protested. 'Obviously it was meant to look that way, eh, A.C.?'

'We have been unable to find Mr. K. London,' the A.C. said. 'If he came and was given the loan, then there is no trace of it in Silver's books and there is no note of the borrower's address, nor of securities he was going to leave.'

'You do not get me, A.C.,' Charles protested. 'I was not suggesting that the unknown London is the guilty party. As Purcell says, it is too obvious. What I was about to ask was: who knew that London had asked for £500 to be waiting for him at 7.30 and did the murderer come earlier than 7.30? And did Silver let him into the house, expecting that he *was* London?'

'The point is well taken,' the chairman said. 'As I understand it the police cannot trace Mr. London. I should consider another version of the incident. There was no address on the London letter, a somewhat unusual omission. I would be inclined to the opinion that the request for a loan was not genuine and was written because the author knew Silver very well, and knowing him was quite certain that he would go to the bank and get the money and would have it in his house.'

The A.C. clapped his hands. 'That, Noël?' he said, 'would support Charles. To know the cupidity of Silver he must know Silver very well personally, and could be a man whom Silver would admit to the house without fear of violence.'

Purcell interrupted. 'I wonder whether we are going on a wrong track,' he said. 'We keep harping on the £500. One person alone, as far as I can recall knew that Silver had £500 — the bank clerk who paid it over. And he is still owing £20 on a £15 loan because, presumably, he had not paid instalments which consequently went on to the capital at compound interest.'

The A.C. nodded.

'Well, were there any more clients heavily in debt to Silver in the same way — desperately in the clutches?'

'There were several, Purcell. But we ourselves have an alibi for them between 7 and 8 o'clock.'

'Have you considered one other point of, it seems to me, great importance,' James asked. 'We are forgetting for the moment the £500. Now the man Eisdale said that Friday was the night Silver received most of his weekly payments — Friday night is mostly work people's pay night. That must have been well known in the neighbourhood. Is it possible that it was this money which the attacker was after — Eisdale said he usually had a lot of money in the house that night — and found to his delight that there was another £500 free, gratis and for nothing?'

The A.C. spread his hands. 'It is a theory,' he said: and left it at that.

The chairman grimaced. 'You aren't helping us much, are you, Edward?' he said. He looked at the professor. 'Come, Stubbs, you are unusually quiet to-night. Surely there is a *logical* explanation to the A.C.'s riddle?'

The professor sat forward. He produced his silver box and took two pinches of snuff from it. He dusted the fallen specks from his lapels — the odd little habit for which the Dilettantes always looked with amused glances. And he spoke:

'Always I w-wait to the l-last,' he said. 'So t-that I may hear your arguments and t-to them apply the p-principles of l-logic.'

'That is so, Professor, and with sometimes devastating effect,' the chairman complimented. 'And to what logical conclusions does Sir Edward's problem to-night lead you?'

The professor put his fingers together and gazed into space. 'It is n-not p-possible that a man can be k-killed at 7.30 o'clock and still be alive at 10.30,' he said.

'Even my logic will extend to that,' Purcell said, humorously.

'Let us examine the matter.' The professor ignored the interruption. 'Sir Edward's surgeon says that d-death occurred at 7.30. But w-what else have we? T-there is a railwayman who c-comes forward not knowing for w-what reason inquiry is being made who s-says he saw the man n-near his home at 10.30. And it m-must be emphasized that Silver w-was not a man to m-mistake for anybody else. Then there is Mr. Eisdale who says — w-what does he say; that Mr. Silver w-was with him from 8 o'clock, that is half an hour after he is s-supposed to be dead, until 10 o'clock.'

The professor looked round and shook his goblin-like shock of hair. He peered through the thick lenses of his spectacles. 'But t-there is something else,' he said. 'I w-would have thought, p-perhaps, that Mr. Eisdale was preparing an alibi w-when he says that the man Silver was with him for t-two hours to 10 o'clock —'

'The porter corroborated the statement,' the chairman reminded him.

'Tsh! A p-porter could be b-bribed to say things, gentlemen. But' — he peered at the A.C. from under his brows — 'but when he said that Silver was with him from 8 to 10 o'clock *he did not know that the railway conductor had already testified to Inspector Edwins t-that he, the c-conductor, had seen t-the old man at 10.30.* Is that not so?' He looked across at the A.C.

'It is so — so far as the evidence goes.'

'Ah! So w-we have a h-honest working-man who saw the old m-man at 10.30, and we h-have a man who sped his p-parting guest at 10 o'clock, and a p-porter who saw the speeding; and we have a d-doctor who says that the old m-man died at 7.30. There is no logic in that, gentlemen.

'There is no logic in t-taking one d-doctor against three m-men who believe the evidence of their eyes. And a d-doctor so often is it n-not is mistaken of the t-time of d-death? I read in the m-medical books that it is impossible for a d-doctor to s-say within two hours either way the actual t-time that a p-person dies who is not found for some time after death, Mr. James,' — and he looked across at the pathologist — 'is t-that not so?'

'Speaking generally, yes, Professor,' the pathologist admitted.

'Ah!'

The A.C. intervened. 'Speaking generally, Professor, Mr. James said. But in certain circumstances the time can be accurately fixed.'

'We will fix it at after 10.30,' the professor said. 'It is logical. Friday n-night, we have h-heard was a night w-when the old man collected his interest on t-the loans. He had, Mr. Eisdale says, a l-lot of m-money on Friday nights. Would he have that money so early as 7.30? If he

h-had not, why should an attacker go there? And, g-gentlemen, would the man or woman, who of course knew those
things go to that house at 7.30 w-when he could not be
c-certain that one or m-more of the man's debtors w-would
not be c-calling on him to p-pay his ill-gotten g-gains.' He
shook his head at the assembled Dilettantes. 'No,' he said,
'it w-was after 10.30 that he d-died and his d-day's money
was taken, and the £500 that was to go to the w-writer of
the letter.'

'Who seems not to have come for the money he wanted
so urgently,' the A.C. said.

'Of course!' Charles said. 'Had he done so he would
have found the old man dead.'

The professor chuckled loudly. 'Oh, it is that Mr.
Charles corroborates me,' he said. 'He died after 7.30.'

38

'You see, the facts d-dovetail, gentlemen.' The professor
beamed behind his thick lenses. 'As t-they must do w-when
the exact science of logical reason is applied to t-them.' He
sat back, satisfaction oozing in chuckles and in the alacrity
with which he partook of two pinches of snuff.

The A.C. smiled. It seemed to the chairman, watching him, that again there appeared about him an air of
distrait, or embarrassment and a lack of *bonhomie* which
usually marked his exposition of a problem. For a moment
he fiddled with the stem of his wineglass, and his monocle
dropped, tinkling, on the glass itself. He seemed to be
thinking; but presently reached a decision.

'I agree, Professor, that facts must fall into a logical
whole when an exact application of scientific investigation
is applied to them. But those facts must have a true foun-

dation — in other words they must be facts. To start from a fallacy is to court disaster — yes, Professor?'

'Undoubtedly,' the professor agreed.

'Which is what has happened in this argument.' Sir Edward paused. He looked round the table. Then:

'Marcus Silver died at, or very near 7.30 o'clock,' he said. 'Of that, to quote Gilbert, there is no possible doubt, no possible doubt whatever. You see, at 6.15 o'clock that night the old woman from upstairs who attended to the wants of Silver took him on a tray a meal of meat and vegetables. At 6.45 she fetched away the tray. The pathologist who conducted the post-mortem found that the distance travelled along the intestines by the eaten food accounted for one hour's digestion, *and only one hour* when digestion was brought to a halt by death. Would you, James, comment on that conclusion?'

The pathologist nodded. 'Digestion is the only completely reliable evidence of time of death *when evidence of the time of the last meal is available,*' he said.

'Then Eisdale was lying when he said that Silver had been with him from 8 to 10 o'clock?' the chairman said.

"He was lying, Noël, yes.'

'And the train conductor was lying when he averred that he saw him at 10.30 near his home? Why? What had he to do with Silver?'

'He was not lying, Noël.'

'And what about the porter who offered to get him a taxi at 10 o'clock?' Purcell asked.

'He was speaking the truth.'

The Dilettantes stared; and there was a moment of baffled silence before the chairman found his voice. 'But the man was dead, you say, at 7.30, Edward.'

The A.C. grinned. 'We will have to apply the professor's Law of Contradiction to the problem, eh Professor?'

he said. He became serious again. 'You know, I, too, have a mind which seeks by logical reasoning the answer to abstruse problems and I will try to practise it now. Not, I am afraid, in the inimitable manner of Professor Stubbs, but at least as well as an apt pupil of his can hope for. I will start with odd circumstances.'

He twisted the cigar in his fingers, and with a regretful glance at it (so it seemed to those watching) placed it still alight in an ash-tray. Then, fingering his monocle with his right hand, he began:

'For some time now, Scotland Yard has been the recipient of congratulations on the successful issue of a number of capital and other serious crimes,' he said. 'While this laudatory view was welcomed, it was at the same time somewhat of a back-handed compliment, for we had not, in fact solved the problems by our sole efforts; the arrests and convictions had been the result of information received. There is nothing unusual in this; Inspector Kenway has told you there is no honour among thieves, and we have 'grasses' and 'narks' who regularly tip us off. What has been unusual in the cases I have referred to is that the information did not come to us from 'narks' or informers. Yet it was complete in every detail necessary to obtain a conviction.' Sir Edward ceased speaking, and, leaning forward refilled his glass from the port decanter; and sipped from it. Then he recommenced. 'Another strange circumstance was that, although most of the offences had been lucrative in plunder, the convicted persons seemed to have gained little from them. To put a long and arduous investigation in a few words we came to the conclusion that there was someone behind all these robberies and crimes, a brilliant mind who, at the same time, had equally brilliantly conceived a safe conduct for himself — at the expense of his operators.

'Now, we succeeded in confirming this by planting undercover men in the prisons in the guise of convicted men. They talked with the real prisoners. And the convicted men talked. But they had no idea of the identity of the man who, they swore, had shopped them. The net result of the experiment was that we were now certain that The Mind used each person once, or at the most twice, and, his usefulness over, gave him away to the authorities, before he had any opportunity to penetrate the identity of his employer. Since the conviction of the operator solved the crime, there were at the time no further police inquiries —'

'Brilliant, Edward!' the chairman commented. 'The man was a bit of a genius.'

'True. And we had had nothing like it before. And it was the more remarkable because few of the operators were really crooks. How they were induced to put themselves in peril we don't know. Probably by blackmail. Now we come to the death of Marcus Silver. I have told you that we had long known him to be a receiver of certain type of property. We watched him unobtrusively, but very thoroughly, after each reported robbery; he neither received any well-known characters nor visited them. So far as we knew he visited only one person, against who we had nothing. We came to the decision that his murder was necessary to remove him as a danger to The Mind. We therefore concluded that by some unfortunate chance he had become the one man who could identify his client; and if he were shopped as others had been he would undoubtedly talk, whereas the others couldn't talk because they had no knowledge of their chief. So he was silenced.

'The murder was skilfully planned and executed. The fact that we know the story is not due to any slip by the murderer; it was the result of something he could not have foreseen and guarded against. And it betrayed him —'

'That w-would be the m-meal at 6.15, w-would it not?' the professor asked. He had been listening intently to the A.C. So much so that he had not once resorted to his snuff box.

'The meal it was,' the A.C. assented. 'Except for that we would certainly have placed death at some time later than 10.30. This is where my logic comes into operation, Professor.'

'In w-what way, Sir Edward?' Stubbs asked.

'*How did it come about that Mr. London did not go for his £500 at 7.30, as he had arranged in the letter?* We know he did not because there was no account of the transaction in Silver's papers.

'The second point of logical contradiction was: *How could a man we knew to be dead at 7.30 come to be seen by a perfectly honest working-man and a porter at 10.30 and 10 o'clock?* It was evident that Silver had not been with Eisdale between 8 and 10 o'clock.

'I will tell you.'

* * *

The Dilettantes were sitting still in their chairs, listening tensely to Sir Edward. Their cigars had gone out, and their glasses still half-filled were untouched. The A.C. leaned forward in his chair; his fingers were still caressing his monocle.

'There never was a Mr. K. London wanting a loan,' he said. 'The letter was written by the murderer to ensure that Silver, in his cupidity, would be in his room at 7.30, and to ensure that the murder would be not only advantageous, but profitable as well — a Machiavellian touch. The murderer visited Silver shortly after 7 o'clock and killed him — killed him easily for he was well-known to his victim.

'He then donned the old man's hat and cloak and, imitating his walk, proceeded to Ealing to the flat of Eisdale, where he was, of course, seen by the porter. At 8 o clock, Eisdale, as himself, went down stairs for cigarettes, thus establishing that he and Silver were in the flat together.

'At 10 o'clock Eisdale re-garbed himself in Silver's cloak, hat and shoes, called downstairs in his own voice: 'Good night, old man. It's a bit late. You'd better get the porter to call a taxi'; and then, closing his door, walked down the stairs as Silver. He made his way to Notting Hill Gate, where he showed himself openly, grunted a reply to the railwayman who greeted him, and re-entered Silver's room. There he divested himself of the cloak and hat, etc., and in the cover of darkness emerged as himself. He went at once to his club, arriving there at his usual time of just before 11 o'clock.'

The A.C. sat back. But he did not relax. 'That is the story of the death of Silver,' he said.

The silence was broken after a minute by the chairman. 'You have arrested Eisdale, then, Edward?' he asked.

'No. Not at the moment. He is absent from his flat. He is so absent on certain nights — and this is one of them. I have no doubt that he will eventually be taken into custody. Yes, Purcell?' He looked at the mathematician who was motioning to speak.

'You intimated some time back, Sir Edward, that information which resulted in the arrests of certain operators of The Mind (as you have called him) did not come from the usual informers. Can we ask how did it come to you?'

The A.C. smiled: and there was steel in his blue eyes as he did so.

'You may ask, Purcell,' he agreed. 'It took us some time to appreciate it. The information was given to us by the man himself gaining access to the Assistant Commissioner of Police of Scotland Yard, and under the cloak of logically arguing a problem told merely his own planning of the crimes.'

He turned to the professor.

'Is there any false premise in my logic, Professor?' he asked.

The professor produced his snuff box. In a silence which hurt, he deliberately took two pinches, replaced the box, and dusted his lapels.

'There is none, Sir Edward,' he said, slowly — and there was no stammer in his voice. 'I, Marcus Stubbs, one-time Professor of Logic, who had an unremunerative Chair at Bonn, say so — and congratulate you.'

He took off his thick-lensed spectacles, and the eyes were those of a man with vision. With a sweep of his right hand he removed his goblin-like hair, and showed a sparsely-covered head, turning grey.

Inspector Kenway moved to his side. 'Marcus Stubbs, alias Herman Eisdale,' he said, 'I arrest you —'

THE END

Made in the USA
Monee, IL
03 March 2020